The Christmas Rat

The Christmas Rat

AVI

Aladdin Paperbacks

New York London Toronto Sydney Singapore

First Aladdin Paperbacks edition October 2002
Text copyright © 2000 by Avi

ALADDIN PAPERBACKS
An imprint of Simon & Schuster
Children's Publishing Division
1230 Avenue of the Americas
New York, NY 10020

Also available in an Atheneum Books for Young Readers hardcover edition.
Book design by Ann Bobco
The text of this book was set in Adobe Caslon.
Printed in the United States of America
10 9 8

The Library of Congress has cataloged the hardcover edition as follows:
Avi, 1937-
The Christmas rat/ Avi.
p. cm.
Summary: Alone in his apartment during Christmas vacation, eleven-year-old Eric finds himself caught in a battle between a strange exterminator and the rat he wants to kill.
ISBN-13: 978-0-689-83842-2 (hc.)
ISBN-10: 0-689-83842-5 (hc.)
[1. Rats—Fiction. 2. Pests—Control—Fiction. 3. Apartment houses—Fiction. 4. Christmas—Fiction. 5. Angels—Fiction.] I. Title.
PZ7.A953 Ch 2000
[Fic]—dc21   99-87429
ISBN-13: 978-0-689-83843-9 (Aladdin pbk.)
ISBN-10: 0-689-83843-3 (Aladdin pbk.)
0410 OFF

For Richard and Katherine

Kids always say they love Christmas vacation. First of all, there's no school, so you get to sleep in and just hang out with friends. Plus, there's lots of staying up late watching rented movies and TV. Then your parents aren't around much because they're busy with work or holiday stuff. And there's candy, too. I mean, tons of it. Finally, there's presents. It really is the best time.

But last Christmas, that's not the way it was. For me, anyway. It was . . . scary.

Friday, December the eighteenth, the day vacation began, was party time in my middle school from morning till three o'clock let-out. Mystery gifts (stupid stuff), dumb games, and all this talk about getting together over the break. At the end of the day it was nothing but, "Call me!" "See ya!" and, "Have a cool yule!"

SIX DAYS BEFORE CHRISTMAS

O*n Saturday it snowed*. I mean, *really* snowed. Deep, white, and clean. A blizzard, I guess. The snow blew so hard you didn't go out unless you had to. I didn't because I had already bought gifts for my parents. Some handkerchiefs for my mom. A scarf for my dad. I know, they weren't so great but, I wanted to be sure I had money left to buy what I really wanted—just in case my folks hadn't paid attention to all the hints I'd dropped.

Only thing was, with both my mother and father having to work weekend Christmas hours—she's a floor manager at Morton's Department Store, he runs a candy shop—there wasn't much for me to do but hang out in our fifth-floor apartment. See, we live in the city.

That day, things were okay. I played some computer games, poked around the Internet, checked my E-mail (nothing), and watched a football game from sunny southern California.

After that, I called my best friend, Pete. I mean, I knew he was supposed to visit his dad in Florida, but I thought maybe the storm had grounded him. But, no, his ma said he had taken off right after school. Anyway, it all meant I sort of did nothing, which is okay on the first day of Christmas break.

But that was only the first day.

FIVE DAYS BEFORE CHRISTMAS

Cold as it was, my mother, father, and I went to church on Sunday morning. To be honest, if it was further than around the corner I bet we wouldn't have gone. I mean, we don't go that often. But at breakfast, my mother, who is sort of sappy about Christmas, said it might do us some good. You know, remind us what the holiday was supposed to be about and all.

Our Lady of Mercy is a nice church, not too big, with these cool stained-glass windows which I like to look at. That morning I didn't really listen to what the minister was saying, except it was all about Mary and the baby Jesus, and (I think) what Mary said to this angel when he told her she was going to have the baby. The minister pointed to one of the windows, where there was the angel (gold wings and white robes) and Mary (blue dress) on her knees before him. It was pretty cool to look at, which I did for most of the service.

Then we went home, and my parents took off for work. I was alone again.

Soon as they left I got on the phone and called Blake, my other best friend. But Blake had to work in his mother's flower shop so he wouldn't be free till after Christmas. I felt like saying, "Who's going to buy flowers in this snow?" But I didn't. Thing is, this was an all-around bummer.

I even called Cory, who was only sort of a friend. His sister said he was in bed with the flu. Double bummer.

Since the weekend before Christmas is the most important shopping time of the year for a lot of people, my parents had to be gone until evening. That meant putting off decorating our tree until Monday night, the only time they could plan on being around.

So there I was, with nothing to do.

To make things worse, even though the snow stopped, the outside temperature dropped way down. I mean, plunged. Everything froze like an old piece of meat in the back of the freezer compartment.

By late afternoon I was bored out of my mind, staring out the living room window onto the icy street below. The parked cars, mostly buried in drifts, reminded me of the backs of whales. For walking, there were only narrow paths that had been dug out through the blowing snow. Daggers of ice hung from doorways, windows, and garbage pails. Sometimes they fell as the wind whipped the streets. I could see them shatter. The few people out were wrapped in coats, caps, mufflers, gloves, and boots. The way they moved reminded me of lost balloons in a stormy sky. I mean, it was one of those days where you think, Hey, I'm snug and safe. Nothing in the world can touch me!

With the tip of my index finger I wrote on the inside frost of the window glass:

MERRY CHRISTMAS!

No one bothered to look up. Then I realized that if they did look, the letters would have read backwards anyway. I supposed if there was one of those Christmas angels flying by—you know, like I'd seen in the church window—maybe he could have read it. But guess what? I didn't exactly see him.

FOUR DAYS BEFORE CHRISTMAS

-1-

Monday morning, *just before* my parents went off to work, a call came saying there would be an exterminator coming. Happened once a year. I think the building where we live arranged for it.

"That's odd," my mother said, when she hung up. "They don't usually come at this time of year."

The thing was, my parents asked me to hang around to let the guy into the apartment. You know, make sure he didn't steal anything while he was going about his business.

"What time is he coming?" I wanted to know.

My dad shrugged. "It's like the phone company.

You have to stay home until they show."

"After he comes," my mom said, "maybe you can bring up the Christmas decorations from the basement." She opened the top drawer of one of the kitchen cabinets and handed me this little key. "The storage bay number is on it." I put the key in my pocket.

"And I promise to bring home a tree tonight," my dad said cheerfully. "A good one."

"We'll decorate," Mom added. "After supper."

Kisses, hugs, and then they left.

It may have been freezing outside but I ate my regular breakfast of cold cereal—a mix of Shredded Wheat and Frosted Flakes—plus a cup of hot chocolate. Sitting alone in the kitchen, I began to think about the vacation ahead. It looked pretty empty and big-time annoying.

I checked my E-mail (nothing), then played some computer games in my room. But after I killed a zillion Zergs it felt like my brain was beginning to itch.

I tried the TV. But, you know, how many kiddie cartoons can you watch? The talk shows were boring too. The cooking shows were all turkey. No decent movies, either. Nothing but screaming Christmas ads. "Buy this! Buy that!" shouted by people with grins so wide you'd think they were selling false teeth.

Mixed in were lots of warnings about the cold snap. "Don't go out unless you have to!"

"If you do go out, bundle up tight!"

"Be careful!"

Then there were, like, all these calls for food, shelter, and clothing for the homeless, the needy, the lonely. "At this time of year . . . the bitter cold . . . "

I got to feeling so antsy, I sneaked a look under my parents' bed to check out my Christmas presents. There was a whole bunch of stuff. Not bad. But their main gift was a disappointment. See, they had gotten me this radio-controlled stunt car, a Rebound 4 x 4 Jet. Thing is, what I'd been hinting at was the Rebound 4 x 4 Jet *Turbo*. It was much better than what they got. It has longer-lasting batteries and goes faster, too.

That made me feel glad that I'd been a bit— hate to say it—cheap with their presents. But with the money I'd saved I could buy the car I wanted, the Turbo, which was the one Pete had. We'd be able to race when he got home from Florida.

It wasn't long before I was sorry I'd looked at my gifts. I mean, what's the point in knowing what your presents are when you can't touch them, use them, or even talk about them? The surprise is, you know, totally gone. I felt like I was waiting for something that had already happened.

By eleven o'clock I was bored stupid. I kept thinking this wasn't the way Christmas was supposed to be. I felt like sticking my head out the window and shouting, "Help! It's the end of the world!"

Then came the knock on our door.

-2-

"Who's there?" I asked. If you live in a city apartment you're always supposed to ask that before you open the door. Even grown-ups do it.

You'd be amazed at the creeps that come into nice buildings like ours.

"Exterminator!" came the answer.

I flipped the dead bolt, plus the second lock, then pulled open the heavy door.

A huge guy was standing before me. I mean, he was really big. Underneath a black peaked cap that had a skull-with-wings logo, he had this straight, white-blond hair that reached to his shoulders. His face was long, pale, with a thin nose and glittering eyes. He had this wild mustache—whitish-blond—that stuck out on both sides of his face. The mustache reminded me of the long-horned cows I'd seen on a school video about the old West.

He was wearing a black leather jacket, fleece-lined. Black combat boots. Army issue, I figured. Each hand gripped the handle of a metal box. The boxes had the same picture of a skull-with-wings as his hat.

There was a smell about him, too. I couldn't place it.

"Folks home?" he asked in a voice that was low, sort of rumbly.

"They're working," I answered, staring up at him. "But they told me you were coming so I can let you in."

"Good," he said.

I stepped aside.

"Where's your kitchen?" he demanded.

"Over here," I said, and led the way.

When we got there the exterminator peered around with those sharp eyes of his. "What you got, dude? Roaches? Mice? Rats?"

"I think we're pretty clean," I said, wondering if he'd be disappointed.

"Nothing to do with cleanliness, kid," he snapped. "If the Queen of England lived around here, trust me, she'd have roaches." He pulled open his metal boxes, laying out canisters marked:

POISON! HARMFUL IF SWALLOWED! CAUTION! CAUSTIC!

"This is the city," he went on, all riled up. "Vermin live here. Fact is, there are more vermin than people. Did you know that, kid?"

"Nope."

"Right. If it weren't for guys like me, the vermin would take over. Have any idea what would happen then?"

I shook my head.

"They would exterminate *people*."

"They would?"

"End of life as you know it. Hey, how come you're not in school?" he suddenly asked, fixing me with a hard stare.

"It's Christmas vacation."

"Wish I had a vacation. For me, it's war all the time. Otherwise the vermin would take over."

While he talked, he'd been busy sprinkling white powder along the base of the kitchen cabinets and inside closets and drawers. His bony, pale fingers opened everything. It was as if he had the right to go into all our hidden places.

I watched him for a while. Then I said, "Do you like your work?"

"Love it."

"How come?"

"People always ask me that," the exterminator

said, without stopping his work with a box labeled *TOXIC!* "See, kid, I was in the military. Special Services. Trained to kill. Guns. Hand-to-hand. Locks. Not a lock in the world I can't open. Booby traps. Mines. Hand bombs. Chemicals. Even bugle blowing—you know, Taps. The works. You name it. That's *all* I knew. I was good at it, too.

"Anyway, I put in my time and then some. I'm not even allowed to tell you what I did. Trust me. I was everywhere.

"But, hey, nothing good lasts forever. Right? It was back to this world for me.

"Didn't take me long to figure out that unless I found a job which would let me kill—legal-like—I'd be in trouble. So I got me a job as an exterminator. It solved everything."

Though all his talk of killing made me feel uncomfortable, I had to admit, he was interesting.

"Hey, I like killing things," he went on as if reading my mind. "And you know what?" He poked a long finger in my direction. "The world likes what I'm doing. And another thing. I get money and respect for what I do."

All I could say was, "Oh."

He had finished the kitchen. "Show me the other rooms," he commanded.

I led the way.

"The hardest thing of all is rats," the exterminator continued. "*The* worst. I can tell you more about rats than you want to know. Filthy creatures. They spread diseases worse than any poison. You wouldn't believe what they steal. Not just small stuff, either."

I must have looked doubtful, because he said, "Hey, in the army, I once saw a rat roll a hand grenade away. They grab things that glitter. Or glow.

"Yeah, people don't know it, but rats have really influenced the world. Sure, sometimes for good, you know, in medical labs. But mostly for the worst. Trust me. Public Enemy Number One. Got any around here?"

"I don't think so."

"People think if you live in a nice neighborhood, no rats. Forget it. I used to work in Beverly Hills. You know, fancy Los Angeles? Huge shopping mall out there for rich folks? Well, it was mostly a resort for rats. Don't worry. I got 'em. Hey, if anyone brings on the end of the world it's going to be me, not them."

He opened one of his boxes and pulled out what I thought was a pistol. Fixed across the barrel at right angles was a miniature bow. It startled me.

"A crossbow," he explained. "I don't believe in using firearms outside the army. Anyway, knowing me," he added with a glare, as if I had just accused him of something, "I'm not so sure I could get a license. But, see, I can fit a bolt in here," he pointed to a slot grooved into the top of the gun barrel, "and shoot. It's pretty silent. Perfect for rats."

I stared at the weapon.

He quickly put the crossbow away, then whipped a business card out of his pocket and handed it to me. The card was red. The letters were printed in black.

Anjela Gabrail
Exterminator
225-5403
24-Hr Cell Phone

"You ever see a rat, kid, ring me. Anytime. Anywhere. Keep my cell phone by my pillow. I'll be there. People call me Anje. You know, An-je. And trust me, I hate rats."

"Yes, sir," I said, putting his card in my pocket.

Anje was in the living room now, kneeling on the floor, fiddling with a canister in the middle of the rug.

"Okay, kid," he went on. "Gas warfare time. I'm setting off this bomb. It'll fog the place with poison, killing the really small vermin. Lethal. Breathe it and it'll make you sick. So get out of here for twenty-five minutes. Or more. Go to a buddy's. Read a comic book in the hall. Anywhere but here. I'll shut the door behind us. Don't come back until time's up. But if you go outside, wrap yourself up tight. It's wicked."

Grabbing my coat, I watched as he twisted the cap off the fog bomb.

There was a hiss. A stream of fog shot into the air. It had a sour smell which I realized was what I had smelled when Anje first walked in.

"Take cover!" he shouted, and began to back away from the spewing bomb.

I ran for the door. The exterminator, steel cases in hand, followed me into the hallway. He slammed the door behind us. Then he unrolled a long strip of masking tape from his pocket and covered the cracks around the door. "Got a watch?" he asked.

"Yes."

"Remember," he said. "Nothing less than twenty-five minutes."

"Twenty-five minutes," I repeated.

"And if you see a rat, call me. You've got my number. You and me, we'll kill him, okay? Merry Christmas!"

"Merry Christmas," I replied.

- 3 -

For a second I watched as Anje went to the next apartment, where our neighbor, old Miss Cromwell, lived. He rapped on the door. As he stood there he glanced over and flashed a thumbs-up sign at me.

I shifted away, and only then did I realize I was stuck in the hallway with nothing to do. I had left the apartment so fast I forgot to bring anything like a book or my Game Boy. I even turned back around, thinking maybe I could help the extermi- nator, but he had gone.

I wandered over to the window at the end of the hall. As always, it was locked shut. I stared down at the street but there was nothing interest- ing to watch.

Checking my wristwatch to see when the twenty-five minutes would be up, I decided I'd go down to the lobby and wait. At least I could sit in one of the soft chairs.

I took the elevator down. It clanked and groaned the way it always does. I can tell which way it's going—up or down—by the noise it makes.

Our lobby has mirrored walls and these long tables where deliveries are left. I checked them out. Some were marked DON'T OPEN TILL CHRISTMAS! A few tinsel decorations had been strung up on the walls. My dad says they're just reminders to tip the building staff.

There were foil icicles on the double lobby doors and a couple of plastic wreaths on the doors to the street. A tin angel blowing a horn had been stuck on the door at the rear of the lobby. That door led to a stairwell you can use to go up (to the apartments) or down (to the basement) if you don't want to take the elevator.

My parents always take the elevator and I like to race them using the steps. Sometimes I push the buttons on each floor so the elevator keeps stopping. That way I always beat them. Once—before they got on—I flipped the OFF switch. The elevator didn't go at all. That made them mad.

Anyway, I sat in one of the lobby chairs, checking my watch a lot. Mostly I kept thinking about the exterminator, what he had said. The more I thought about him, the weirder he seemed. But, you know, interesting. I mean, I sort of liked him.

I guessed it was a good thing he was doing. But were all the vermin so bad that it had to be—like he said—a *war?* I wondered if the vermin felt the way he did.

Before five minutes were up I was so restless I

decided to go outside. Not that I had any particular place to go. I hadn't brought any money. But hitting the street seemed better than sitting in the lobby doing nothing. I told myself the fresh air would be good for me. But when I stepped out through the front doors the cold hit me so hard, I gasped. My lungs actually stung. Like, the cold was totally worse than I'd expected. Still, I buttoned up my coat and set out to walk around the block.

I plunged my hands deep into my pockets and felt the key my mother had given me for our storage bay. Moving into the wind, I kept my head bent, eyes down, listening to the crunch my feet made as I walked in the snow. Some places where people had shoveled were okay, but narrow. Other places were bumpy with ice.

I walked as fast as I could. There was no one else on our block. The further I went, the more I thought how great it was going to be to get inside again. I promised myself another hot chocolate and a thick comforter. I'd be glad to be home. I mean, in a way, I wasn't sorry I'd come out because now I knew how good it would be to stay in.

I was just about back to our building when I remembered the Christmas decorations. I figured I could kill some more time by getting them from the basement.

Rubbing my icy hands I pushed through the back lobby door and headed down.

In the public places of our building, which is called The Eden Apartments, there's all this soft lighting on walls painted light green, pink, and blue. In the basement there's no color at all. Just cement, plus a couple of places with dirt. They must have poured the cement wrong or something. The light comes from weak, bare bulbs that dangle from black wires. The air feels chilly and dank and there's this white, chalky dust all over. Anytime I'd been there it made me think of a place where people are buried. A crypt. I mean, if our building was named after the Garden of Eden, what was this place?

Actually, I had been in the basement only a few times since we moved into the apartment three years ago. That was when we were in and out of our storage bin. To tell the truth, I felt a little nervous being down there. It's pretty depressing.

The thing is, the whole area is mazelike. Corridors lead every which way and the ceilings are low, crisscrossed with white pipes and electrical wires. Along one wall is a row of big metal cans full of incinerated garbage.

There are a few solid doors. I think they're made of steel. One is labeled ELECTRICAL. Another is TELEPHONE. A third says FURNACE.

There are all these storage bays built into a wall. When you move into the apartment you can ask for a bay. That's what we did. They each have steel screen doors with locks. Makes 'em look like cages. You can see through these doors, but you can't get in without a key. Or out, I guess. Most of them were full. There were cardboard boxes in one, trunks in another, lawn chairs in another. I even saw a cool kayak.

Feeling slightly nervous about being there, I walked slowly and softly to our own bin, #13. My steps sounded pretty loud on the concrete.

I used the key in the lock on the mesh door. It swung open stiffly and I stepped inside. The place wasn't much more than a big closet. There were stacked and numbered cardboard boxes. That was my dad's neat way. There was also a baby's high chair and a folding bed. Mine, I guessed.

As for the cardboard boxes, the problem was you had to know what the numbers meant to know what was inside.

I pulled open one box. I found a lot of baby clothes inside. Another box had what I think were old checks and papers. A third had nothing but photographs. I kept looking.

I think it was the ninth box. When I opened it I saw our Christmas decorations—bulbs, electric lights, decorations, other stuff. And right in the middle of it all was this huge rat.

– 4 –

The rat was about a foot long and totally scrawny. He was gray-brown in color, with a long, thin, naked-looking tail. I could see his bristling whiskers. His eyes were bright and black. As I looked at him, he looked right back at me, his snout sniffing the air. Like, checking me out.

Right beside him was this old-fashioned pasteboard angel we always put on the top of the tree. Something my mother had saved since she was a little girl.

The rat had been eating it.

When I opened the box I almost died. Seriously. See, I remembered what the exterminator had said, that rats were "the absolute worst. Human enemy number one." I felt really freaked.

As I jerked away from him, the rat ran up against my side of the box, one little paw on the box edge. Facing me, he stood up on his hind legs, clawing the air as if in a rage. He suddenly jumped up and out. I staggered back while he scrambled down the side of the box and took a flying leap to the floor. Then he raced for the open bay door, and whipped down the corridor.

I ran out after him, just catching a glimpse as he disappeared around a turn. I didn't follow. Couldn't. I was too scared. I just stood there, heart pounding like crazy.

After a bit I went back to the bay, nervous that maybe there were more rats. I jiggled the decoration box, waited, looked. Nothing. Finally, I picked up the box, shut the bay door, locked it, and took the elevator up to the fifth floor. When I got there I checked my wristwatch. The twenty-five minutes weren't up, so I put the box down and sat up against the wall, glad for the moment to calm my jitters. But I kept thinking about that rat. I mean, how did he even get into our stuff?

Hearing a sound, I looked around fast. It was the exterminator. He was staring down at me.

"Hey, kid," he boomed, "it's okay now. You can go back inside. You'll be fine."

"Mr. Anje . . ."

"What's up, kid?"

"I . . . I saw a rat."

His face turned red. His eyes narrowed. His mustache ends seemed to stiffen. It was as if I had just insulted him. "You telling the truth?" he demanded.

"Yeah," I said.

"In *this* building?"

"I just saw it. In the basement. In our Christmas box."

To prove it, I stood up, opened the box, and held up the angel the rat had been chewing.

Anje took it from my hand, gazed at it, examining it on all sides as if he were checking out what had been eaten away. He didn't look too happy.

"We need to talk," he said, handing back the angel and peeling the masking tape off our door with a sharp ripping sound.

I led the exterminator back inside. The apartment air stank of the poisonous fog. He marched right down to the living room and opened a window. "Might be cold for a bit," he said. "But that stuff can kill you."

I left the box of decorations in the living room, and the two of us sat down at the kitchen table.

"Now the thing with rats is," he began, flipping back his long hair away from his face, "you have to know where they live. Their nest. No point in getting just one. They breed like bandits."

"I don't know anything about this one," I confessed. "When I first saw him, he was in that box of Christmas things. Like I said, eating that angel.

"I was supposed to bring up the decorations," I

went on. "So we can do our tree tonight." Then I said, "Maybe the rat was just getting out of the cold."

"Exactly," Anje agreed. "A rat is a creature of opportunity. He would head right for the basement. Where it'll be warm and dark. Maybe a little damp. They store garbage down there?"

"It's burnt. So it's just the ashes."

"Hey, any way they can get it. They thrive on the stuff. Okay. Here's what you need to do. Get back into the basement. Like I said, that's where he'll most likely stay. Reconnoiter. Find where he's hunkering down. Are the lights always on down there?"

"I think so."

"Okay. This time, when you go down, get the lights off. Use a flashlight. You got one?"

"I don't know."

"I'll lend you one." He dipped into one of his metal boxes and handed me what looked like an ordinary, cheap white plastic flashlight. It was small. Not much bigger than my hand. On its side, in gold letters, was his name: Anjela Gabrail.

I took it.

"Okay," the exterminator said. "Use this. But when you're down there, just make sure you keep your eyes open. Walk quietly. Stay alert. Work out the lay of the land. Remember, they are really nasty. If cornered, a rat will attack. But that light should protect you. Okay, can you do all that?"

I swallowed hard. "Yes, sir."

"You'll be my deputy. What's your name?"

"Eric. Eric Andrick."

"Okay, Eric, you really with me on this?"

"Yeah, I guess so," I said, adding, "got nothing better to do."

He stiffened and looked at me hard. "Well, you got something now. Raise your right hand."

I wasn't sure what he was getting at but I did as I was told.

"Do you swear to oppose and attack all rats in your vicinity, so help you God?"

"Sure," I said.

"Or pay the penalty?"

"What's the penalty?"

"Just say it, kid."

"Or pay the penalty."

He glared at me. "Buddy, you're supposed to say, 'So help me God.'"

"So help me God."

"You're in."

I thought of asking, "In *what?*" but I didn't.

He stood up. "Okay, Eric. Don't worry. Hey, you still got my business card?"

"Yes, sir."

"Forget sir. Call me Anje. When you get more information, call me. Day or night. For rats, I'm on twenty-four hour alert."

"Cool."

"We'll get him." He held out a hand. I felt I had to shake it. His grasp was cold and even hurt a little.

"Let's see," Anje went on. "Christmas is Friday. Okay, that's our target date. Our mission is to make sure that rat doesn't enjoy Christmas. Yeah, he'll be our Christmas rat. Okay?"

"Okay."

I let the exterminator out. Before leaving, he saluted me. "Code name . . . this building have a name?"

"The Eden Apartments."

"Okay, code name for the operation is Eden . . . trap. Got it? Eden trap."

"Yes, sir. Eden trap."

"Roger and out. I'll expect a report this evening." He marched off. Before turning a bend in the hallway, he saluted again. It was like I'd been taken into the army. His army.

-5-

I double-bolted the door. The stink of the poison fog still hung in the air. Bitter. And it made my nose itch. Still, the apartment was so cold I shut the living room window.

I went into the kitchen and, with a comforter wrapped around me, I thought over what had happened.

That rat was so creepy. Just to think about him made me a little queasy. And when I thought about Anje . . . I mean, the guy was really fierce. Sort of angry. When I had told him about the rat he, like, took it personally. As if I insulted God or something. But, as I thought about it, I sort of agreed with him. You had to get rid of rats. You couldn't have them where people live, right? Besides, I didn't have anything better to do. In fact, I got to thinking that there was no point in waiting until nighttime to reconnoiter. I liked the word. It sounded strong, full of action. What I needed.

Making sure I had the apartment key in my pocket, I grabbed the little flashlight Anje gave me, clicking it on to see if it worked. It did, but in an odd sort of way. It wasn't just the front part that shot a beam and all. The whole thing glowed. Cool.

I took the elevator down to the basement.

When I got there the lights were off. I mean, that sucker was dark, totally dark. I did wonder for a second how come the lights had been on before, and were off now. But I didn't spend a bunch of time thinking about it. Besides, Anje had said it would be better if it was dark. So I just flicked on the flashlight. There was a beam all right, but like I said, the whole thing glowed too.

I started off down the corridors, past the wall of

storage bays, then around what I remembered was the turn the rat had taken. In all that dark, it was really confusing. So I moved slowly, poking the beam of the flashlight into any corner I saw, almost scared about what I might find. The glow of the flashlight case made me feel like I was in some sort of cocoon. Made me feel safer.

Then, suddenly, I saw the rat on the top of a large canister labeled CLEANING SOLVENT.

He was up on his hind legs like a dog begging, those tiny, pink-clawed paws of his waving in the air. All the while he was squeaking, opening and closing his mouth wide so that I could see his chisel-like, yellow front teeth. It was like he was making a speech. Not that I understood anything.

I stared at him, fascinated and, you know, scared. From my light I guess he knew I was there because he seemed to be looking right back at me with those bright black eyes. At the same time he kept clawing the air as if he was pulling in invisible threads. Or climbing a net.

The next second the rat leaped off the canister,

landing close to where I stood. I jumped back.

He stood up on his hind legs, then dropped to all fours and began to scurry along the floor at the base of the wall. After a brief moment of being shocked, I ran after him.

Let me tell you something. That rat was fast, a lot faster than me. But my flashlight gave me enough light—and the corridor was long enough—so that I could follow him, catching glimpses of that long naked tail of his as he zipped around corners.

All of a sudden I was facing a dead end. The rat was at the far end, sniffing frantically along the walls. He was squeaking too, like he was searching for an escape route or something. I mean, real panicky. He even began scratching at the floor. At one of those dirt spots. Suddenly he stopped, looked up, fixed his beady eyes on me and just stood there, absolutely still, except for his quivering nose. Once, twice, he let out sharp squeaks.

The thing is, I had trapped him. He must have realized it, too. But I didn't know what to do about it.

All of a sudden, he dove at me. Like he was

attacking me. Freaked, I leaped back and pressed myself against the wall.

The next instant he was on me. I mean, I could feel his small feet galloping over my sneakers. Then he was off in a shot, and, as my flashlight beam played about, I watched him dash along the corridor and vanish into the dark.

I didn't follow. I couldn't. My heart was pounding too fast. I was finding it hard to breathe. I had to lean against the cement wall for a minute. As I did I had this feeling come over me, like I had failed at something because, I have to admit, I was really glad he was gone.

After I calmed down, I made it back to the elevator, the flashlight marking my way. The beam was still working. But the flashlight case had stopped glowing. Not that I cared. I was just glad I didn't see the rat, not one sign of him, as I inched back to the elevator. Once I got to our apartment, I made sure I locked myself in. Tight.

6

Sitting on our living room couch, I thought over what had happened. I mean, I was pretty upset. I kept wondering what the rat was doing in the building. Was he just getting out of the cold? Was there such a thing as a homeless rat? Was he alone? Or would there be more of them? Did he have family? Was he intending to stay? Was he as bad as Anje the exterminator had said?

Then I got to thinking about how brave the rat had been. After all, I was probably huge-looking. Maybe he thought I was coming at him. Which in a way I was. I tried to imagine how I might have looked, like some giant, I suppose. Was he scared? I wondered. Did he know I was? And, I asked myself, what did being freaked by a rat say about me, an eleven-year-old kid? Was I normal?

I mean, I had all these questions but no answers.

Still, I kept coming back to the main question: What was I supposed to *do* about him?

That's when I fished Anje's red business card

from my pocket and called his cell phone number. A recorded message told me to leave my phone number and a simple message. I did. My message was, "Eden trap."

I don't think it took five minutes before a call came in.

"Gabrail here!"

"Anje?"

"Yeah."

"It's me, Eric, the boy from the Eden Apartments. Five-B. You know, the one who saw the rat. I went to the basement like you said. I found him."

"Good job!" he cried. "You kill him?"

"I . . . chased him but he got away," I said apologetically.

"Hey, don't worry about it. They're scary."

That made me feel better.

"Look," Anje went on, "I'm still around your building. Meet me in the basement." He hung up.

I don't know where Anje had been but he was waiting for me when I got down there. He was holding one of his steel boxes and this humongous black flashlight. Which was a good thing because the lights were still off and I forgot to bring the flashlight he gave me. As I stepped out of the elevator, he offered a crisp salute. "You did good, kid!" he snapped.

I smiled stupidly. I really didn't think I had been good but I was glad he thought so.

"Show me where you saw him," he said.

It took a while to find the place where I had cornered the rat. But being with Anje made the whole scene less scary.

When we got there I pointed to the dead end area. "There," I said. You could see where the rat had been at work in the dirt—except the hole was bigger than I had remembered.

"Not bad," Anje said. "You had him cold. Good strategy, bad tactics. I mean, you got him where you wanted him, up against a dead end, but you didn't have the right firepower."

"Firepower?"

"If you had an M-16 assault rifle, hey, no problem. Blast him to nothing. Wouldn't be a hair left. Not a smear. He'd be in rat hell right now. Burning."

I glanced up at Anje. He was so huge, with that long blond hair and mustache. I was glad he was there, but at the same time he was making me suddenly feel uncomfortable.

"Failing firepower, there's always my crossbow," he went on. He removed it from his box.

Fascinated, I watched as he positioned a brass bolt with an iron tip—it was like a small arrow without feathers—into a slot along the top of the weapon.

I automatically stepped away.

He cocked the thing by pulling the bow back. It made a distinct *click*. Then he aimed the weapon at the concrete wall and pulled the trigger. The bow made a high-pitched twanging sound.

Thwack.

"See," Anje said.

I looked where he pointed. The bolt was sticking right out of the wall. I mean, it had gone *into* the cement about an inch. Awesome.

At the same time, I began to feel a little sympathy for the rat. I mean, Anje was right, that shot would have turned him into a bunch of nothing.

All I said, though, was, "What do we do now?"

Anje yanked the bolt from the wall and put his crossbow back in his box.

"Traps," he said. "Traps will bust his back. Or maybe poison, which is cleaner. Look here." He pointed to the floor. "That rat found a weak spot and was trying to dig a hole."

"Maybe there's cement under the dirt."

"Nothing stops a rat. Come on, let's inspect some more."

He led the way, his powerful beam poking and probing like a light sword into dark corners. I came along cautiously, looking around him, trying to see what he was seeing.

When we reached the elevator again, he paused.

"Difficult terrain," he said. "But not impossible. Got the flashlight I gave you?" he asked.

"In the apartment."

"Hey, you want to keep it with you at all times. If you don't have the right equipment—we call them *assets* in the military—you never can win."

"Win?"

"Got to get our Christmas rat, don't we?"

"I suppose . . . "

"The thing is," he said, fixing me with an angry glare, "you tell someone he's dead, and if you don't follow through, he's gonna live forever."

"Someone?"

"The rat, bud. Who'd you think?" He looked around, waved his flashlight. When he caught sight of the door marked ELECTRICAL, he pulled at it. It was locked but that didn't bother him. He dipped into a steel box again and pulled out a big ring of maybe a zillion keys. He studied the lock, flicked through his keys and had the door open in seconds.

"See," he said, "I can open anything."

I looked up at him.

"Yeah," he added, with the closest thing to a smile I had seen from him. "Even your apartment."

Inside the electrical room—which was small—there were three walls covered with switch panels.

Anje probed them with his flashlight beam. "Okay, here we are. See," he said, pointing to a label that read BASEMENT LIGHTS. He reached out and flicked the switch. The basement lights went on.

"What you need to do is turn the overhead stuff off," Anje explained. "Rats like darkness. So, make the enemy think you're meeting them on their terms. Then overpower them where they think they're strong. It doesn't just flatten them, it demoralizes them. Get it?"

"I think so."

"Fine. Okay, Eric—do I have the name right?"

"Yes."

"Still with me?"

"Yeah."

"Bored?"

"Not now."

"Here are your orders. Get yourself down here in the middle of the night. Say, two A.M. Rat time. Turn off the lights. Here." He touched the right switches. "Head back into that dead end area where the rat was digging and set yourself up. Keep that flashlight I gave you at hand. Then wait. Be patient. Make sure he's really trying to dig in. Report back and, trust me, that rat's standing in front of his god awaiting judgment. Remember our mission: a dead rat by Christmas. We together on that, dude?"

"Yes . . . sir," I said, a little unnerved.

7

In the apartment again I sat at the kitchen table and ate my lunch, a ham sandwich, soda, and a bag of chips. I could still smell some of that poison fog. Even a whiff of it made my nose itch. The exterminator's white flashlight was on the table before me. When I picked it up it started to glow like it had before. I put it down and the glow faded. Loose connection, I figured.

As I ate, I thought about Anje's orders. I mean, the guy was really determined. But I allowed myself to admit that he was a little spooky too.

The phone rang.

"Hi, sweetie." It was my mother's cheerful voice. "How you doing?"

"All right."

"The exterminator come yet?"

"Yeah."

"Everything okay?"

"Place smells kind of funny."

"I know. Wish they hadn't come just before Christmas. They never did before. What are you doing, hon?"

"Just hanging around."

"No friends?"

"In Florida. Or busy. Or sick."

"Christmas in four days, sweetie. Think presents!"

I remembered the wrong radio-controlled car they had gotten me. "Yeah," I murmured.

"You sound bored."

"A little."

She sighed. "Eric, honey, read a book. Watch television. Video games. Draw pictures. This is vacation time. You can do whatever you want. I'll tell you, I could go for a little of that."

"I know."

"It's frantic here. Don't know when I can get to lunch. Did you remember to bring the decorations up?"

"Yeah."

"Wonderful. We'll do the tree tonight. What would you like for dinner?"

"Macaroni and cheese."

"You got it. Have to run. Love you, sweetie."

"Bye."

I went into my room and found a book to read. It didn't interest me. I came back to the living room, switched on the TV. Everybody was stupid. I calculated how many hours till Christmas. Something like eighty. How many minutes. Four thousand, eight hundred. Boring!

I sat for a while but got uncomfortable with the stillness. My mind kept turning to the rat. And Anje. Feeling a little nervous, but also figuring I should do *something*, I picked up Anje's flashlight and took the elevator back down to the basement. I mean, I knew I was supposed to go to the basement at night. Two A.M., he had said. Except no way I was going to do that then.

On the way down I had this weird thought: I had never seen anyone else there. It was like going down into the land of the dead. Then I reminded myself that I had seen Anje down there. And he was alive, right?

8

When I stepped into the basement, I found the lights on. That was good because the place felt deserted. Then, as I stood there, the elevator doors slid shut behind me. It began to clank up and the familiar noise slowly drifted away. All that was left was me with a heart beating too fast.

I stood still for a long time, Anje's glowing flashlight in my hand. Part of me wanted to go back up and forget the whole business. The other part kept me there. I mean, this was the most boring week in my whole life. Okay, I told myself, go find the rat. I mean, it was something to do and if the rat could do harm . . .

I went to the door marked ELECTRICAL, and just stood there like a jerk, asking myself if it would be locked. But when I finally tried the door, it opened. I was sure it had been locked before. Was that Anje's doing? I wondered. I mean, he said he could open any lock in the building.

Anyway, I pulled the door wide and looked into the small room. I had been there only a short time before but the walls seemed covered with more switches than I remembered. After some searching I found the three labeled BASEMENT LIGHTS. And flipped them.

The lights all went out. I flicked the flashlight on. The whole thing glowed again.

Cautiously, I began to wander about, pointing the light beam on the floor, the walls, even the ceiling.

Somehow the basement seemed bigger than I had remembered it. I mean, it was totally quiet. More mazelike, too. A whole lot of emptiness. So there was nothing to do but wander.

I found myself in the same dead end where I had cornered the rat. I knew this was the place because I found the hole the rat had been digging. The thing is, it looked bigger. Maybe he was making a home for other rats. Or then again, I suppose he could have been just trying to get away. The point is, I didn't know what he was doing.

I examined the hole close up but since I was nervous about putting my hand into it, it was hard to tell how deep it went. The real question was, would he come back to this spot?

I moved along the wall a few paces then sat down, leaned back, and turned off the flashlight. I was real glad then for its faint glow. Made me feel better.

But only a little. I hugged my knees close to my body, keeping a finger on the flashlight switch, just in case. I mean, that dark beyond the glow was really intense.

As I waited I got to thinking how, outside, it was white with snow and cold. Inside, it was black and warm. Still, I shivered. What would I do if I heard the rat? I reminded myself that my job was only to find out where he hid. No more. Then Anje could take care of . . . killing him.

The words—which I had heard in my head—sort of echoed and re-echoed along the corridors of the basement. *Killing him.* Killing . . . I began to wonder how come I got into this thing. Because the rat was bad, an enemy to humans. Because it was Christmas vacation and I had nothing to do. Then I thought about it being Christmas, and you know, all that stuff about Jesus being born, and there I was, trying to kill a rat. Something was wrong.

With a sigh I leaned my head back and closed my eyes. Compared to the basement darkness, I liked my own shut-eyed darkness better. I got to thinking I needed to know more about rats. Maybe, I told myself, I should go to the library.

I let my mind go blank.

Except, the next moment I heard this faint noise. Or had I? Holding my breath, I listened to the stillness. I mean, it was *really* still. Was someone else coming down into the basement?

"Hello!" I shouted. "*Hello!*"

No answer. I waited some more. I don't know how long, but sure enough, the first sound came again. It was tiny, like the sound of little feet scurrying. Was it the rat? My heart began pounding again. I think it was then that I had this thought: *Maybe the rat is hunting* me.

The sound came again, closer, louder. I couldn't be sure where it was coming from. But I positively heard the squeaking sound. Sort of like small rusty wheels turning, turning, rolling toward me.

I looked down. The flashlight was glowing. It was then that I wondered: What if the rat was moving toward that glow? You know, maybe it was *attracted* to the flashlight.

I quickly stuffed it under my shirt, but small as the flashlight was, the glow came through. I put my hand over it, but what happened was, my hand turned red—bloodred.

And the squeaky sound kept coming closer.

Beginning to feel panicky, I shifted my head, first one way, then another, trying to track the sound. When the squeaking grew louder, I was convinced it was off to my left, where I had seen the rat before. Hands shaking, I aimed the flashlight toward the sound and flicked the switch.

The beam of light punched a hole in the darkness. At the very end of the hole was the rat. His head was up, sniffing. His eyes appeared to be on fire.

I freaked. I mean, I really jumped, making a lot of noise. When I looked again, the rat was gone.

Pushing myself against the wall, I swept the beam of light back and forth, trying to spot him. I couldn't. I didn't care. Wanting to get out of there, I stood slowly and began to back away toward the electrical room.

Once there, my fumbling fingers turned on the overhead lights. Dazzled by their brightness, I hurried to the elevator, and the apartment. But even there, I didn't feel completely safe. I got into my bed and burrowed down under the blankets. The truth is, I felt sick, cold, and really scared.

It took a while but I calmed down and tried to decide why I felt so bad. Had the rat frightened me? Yeah, sure. That was obvious. But there was more. At first I couldn't get it right. I kept asking myself, was there something wrong with *me?* I mean, was it wrong what I was doing? I really wished Pete was around.

I called his house, thinking maybe his mother would tell me how I could call him. But the phone rang and rang until I finally hung up. Usually the answering machine was on, but not this time.

I think it was about three in the afternoon when I made up my mind that I really had to find out more about rats. Like, maybe the exterminator was wrong. Maybe rats weren't so bad. Anyway, what had the rat done to me? Just because *Anje* said they were bad didn't make it true. I mean, who was *he* to say, you live, you die? Some god or something?

9

I headed for my computer, thinking I'd look up some stuff on rats on the Internet. But then I realized I really wanted to get away from the building.

Bundling myself up, I set off for the library, glad for the excuse to get out. I did leave a note for my parents saying where I had gone in case they got home before I did.

It was a long walk to the library—twelve blocks—and the air was colder than before. It was darker, too, but more people were out on the streets. I could hear them saying, "Merry Christmas!" After twelve blocks my teeth were chattering.

The library was an old building built of red brick and covered with city grime. It wasn't very nice-looking. Inside, though, it was warm and calming. There were only a few people there—except for the children's room where there was this circle of little kids listening to a reading of *'Twas the Night Before Christmas*.

I made my way to the information desk and told the librarian at a terminal there that I wanted information on rats.

She looked up and smiled. "Laboratory rats? Pet rats? Street rats?"

"Street rats . . . I guess."

"Ah!" she said cheerfully. "The nefarious brown rat. I think I can help you." She pushed herself away from her desk.

She went along some low shelves—me following—and grabbed hold of a large volume. "*Encyclopedia of Mammals*," she whispered. She lay the book down, opened it, flipped some pages, and stepped away. "There you are." She went back to her desk.

Left alone, I examined the color plate in the center of the page. It sure looked like my rat. Brown, with a naked tail. A fast reading told me that full-grown rats could be twelve to eighteen inches long. They could weigh more than a pound.

They ate, the book said, "almost anything." They were smart. They bred fast. They were born naked, blind, and helpless.

My rat wasn't helpless.

Then there was this whole page about rats and history. Like Anje had said, they really were important. Rats and people seemed to go together lots, sometimes in good ways, sometimes bad. The worst was something called the Black Death, which happened in the thirteen hundreds. You'd get lumps on your body. There were spots, boils, and pain, too. You'd stink, then die, fast. Millions of people did die all over the world. And rats brought it. Made me sick to read about it.

But even though rats brought diseases they were used—in laboratories—to learn how to fight diseases. Made me wonder: Did they fight the diseases they brought? I mean, how could they be both things at once?

I read a little more but it was too creepy. I left the library and headed back. It was nighttime now and there were more people on the streets. Coming home from work, I figured, trudging through the snow, heads down against the cold. Were they going to find rats in their buildings? Were those rats connected to my Christmas rat?

Though what I had learned disgusted me, there was this big question that kept going through my head. Did I want to kill my rat or not? At the moment all I knew was that I wanted to be home.

I started to run, almost slipped on some ice, made myself slow down, but still walked as fast as I could, hands deep in pockets, my breath steaming in front of me. I actually found myself wishing there was school tomorrow.

To my relief my mother was home and busy in the kitchen. The apartment was full of cooking smells. They made me realize just how hungry I was—and, finally, safe.

Not that I knew exactly what I was feeling safe from. Was it the rat? Or—I kept asking myself—was it Anje, the exterminator?

Then my father came home with a nice Christmas tree and a wooden stand. The tree was taller than he was, and so plump it was hard to see him behind it. Made me laugh. I was feeling better and better. *This* was what Christmas was really about, like the Christmases I remembered. The ones without Anje.

-10-

During our dinner of macaroni and cheese I wanted to tell my parents about the rat. But I didn't.

Finally, my mother said, "What were you doing at the library?" I realized she must have found my note.

I shrugged. "Looking for a book."

"You find it?"

"It was out."

She didn't ask any more.

Later on, I asked myself why I hadn't told them about the rat. I decided I needed to figure out what I thought of it all first.

We decorated the Christmas tree that night. It wasn't as big as some years, but my father still needed help setting it on the wooden stand. It slanted only a little bit. I helped him drape the lights, too. A few bulbs were out, but the whole thing looked cool.

With Christmas carols playing, my mother made popcorn. She had gotten some cranberries, too, and we strung them into long Christmas necklaces and draped them around the tree.

Finally there were decorations, old ones from my grandparents' trees. Glass ornaments and such. The only one bad moment came when my mother discovered that her treetop angel had been chewed. I mean, she was totally upset. See, she had kept that angel since she was a little girl. "Oh, Eric," she cried, teary, "I wanted to give it to your children. It was kind of my guardian angel."

"How come you kept it packed away?" I asked.

My question seemed to surprise her. "It's a Christmas angel," she replied as if that answered it.

"We'll find another," my father told her.

She said, "It won't be the same."

"Then we'll get this one fixed," he offered. "I suppose even angels need attention from time to time." Once again, I wanted to tell them about the rat but I didn't.

Standing on tiptoes, my mother put her partly chewed angel on the treetop. She gave a sad smile. "Maybe we should get a better one. Start a new tradition."

As we always did after we decorated, we put out a few presents, the ones that came from relatives. There were two from Aunt Thelma who lived in Texas, one from Uncle Willie in Massachusetts. They always sent the same things. T-shirts from Aunt Thelma that bragged DON'T MESS WITH TEXAS. From Uncle Willie, a box of chocolates shaped like Christmas wreaths. Willie was my father's brother, and of course he knew my dad had a candy store. It was Uncle Willie's idea of a joke, but the present had always annoyed my dad. My mother would say every year, "Now Lloyd, it's Christmastime. Be loving." And my dad would shrug. Always happened just that way, for as long as I could remember.

Then, to make it all complete, we hung my stocking. It was made of red felt and had faint green sparkles on it spelling out "Merry Christmas." I had hung that stocking since I was five years old. I knew I was a little big for that sort of thing, but I liked it. So did my folks.

My mother made herb tea for us and served chocolate-chip cookies. Then we watched the news and got a lot of stupid talk about the cold snap. They kept asking the same question: "How low will the temperature go?"

"It's keeping everyone inside," my father said, thinking, I guessed, about his store. "Not good for sales. They'll be down this season."

"People have to buy candy," my mother replied encouragingly. "It's Christmas, after all," she added. "Can't have Christmas without sweetness."

"It's bitter outside," my father said, making a face. "Not a creature is stirring."

That got me feeling very tired. I announced I was going to bed.

First my mother came in to kiss me good-night, then my father.

"Dad," I called out just as he was about to leave the room, "what do you think about rats?"

He turned back. "I suppose I don't like them much. But I've been told they make great pets. What makes you ask?"

"Just thinking."

He sat on the end of my bed. "Here it's almost Christmas and you're thinking about rats. Some TV movie you saw?"

"A story I read."

He smiled. "Hey, reading can get the mind going. Good-night, son."

"'Night, Dad."

I had wanted to read. Anything but think about rats. I couldn't. According to Anje I was supposed to go into the basement that night and search around.

I turned off my bedside lamp. The hall light was still on and my door was partially open so it wasn't completely dark.

As I lay there I thought again about who was more creepy: the rat or Anje the exterminator? The question made me toss and turn. It was as if I knew the answer, but didn't want to admit it.

"The exterminator," I finally said out loud. The moment I spoke the words, I had a flood of bad feelings about Anje: How uncomfortable he made me. All that talk of killing. His hard eyes. Long, white-blond hair. The skull-with-wings on his hat. His poison boxes. His blunt, bossy way of talking. Acting like he was the judge of the whole world. Sure, the rat was creepy. He, I decided, was worse.

Just allowing myself these thoughts made me feel better. Like a window had been opened, the poison gone.

I shifted under my covers, closed my eyes and waited for sleep. It didn't come. The relief I'd felt lasted only moments. I got nervous all over again. See, I started thinking—what would Anje say when he knew I was bothered more by him than the rat? I just knew he would know. Would he think of me as a traitor to humans? Would he turn on me? Would the rat be killed anyway?

I rolled over in bed, searching for a more comfortable position. The truth was, I didn't want the rat to be killed. I mean, the rat wasn't bothering me. Just because Anje said he should be killed didn't mean . . . anything.

There it was, *why kill anything?* And, you know, it was Christmastime.

No way, I told myself. I wouldn't do it.

Except, the next question was, should I call Anje and tell him what I'd decided?

No—he'd know. I knew he would. And it was his reaction I dreaded.

I didn't want to think about any of that. Instead, I turned on my lamp and read until I grew drowsy. Christmas, I reminded myself, was only three days away. I wished it would hurry. I started to hum *Silent Night*. Somewhere in the middle of it I fell asleep.

THREE DAYS BEFORE CHRISTMAS

-1-

Tuesday *morning, I woke* up late. My parents had already gone to work. On the kitchen table I found a note:

> **Eric,**
> **Didn't want to wake you. You looked so peaceful! Try to *do* something today. Call a friend. See a movie! The 14th Street Arcade? Here's ten bucks to help things along. If you go somewhere, give one of us a call so we'll know where you are.**
> **Love, Dad**
> *P.S. Still very cold! Bundle up well!*

The bottom part was in my mother's handwriting.

As I ate breakfast I read the note over. Pushing my food aside—I didn't eat much—I thought about what movie I wanted to see. There was a place on 4th Avenue that showed eight different ones. I probably could find something I wanted to see.

Had I ever gone to a movie alone? I didn't think so. I wondered if Cory was over the flu. Though I doubted it, I decided it was worth a call.

I showered, got dressed, and was about to make my call when the doorbell rang.

From inside I shouted, "Who is it?"

"Eden trap."

"What?"

"Eden trap. The rat. It's me, Anje. You forget?"

"Oh." My heart sank. I had put the rat business out of my mind. Now it was back. *He* was back. Along with all my thoughts from the night before, only worse. I felt I had to open the door.

There he was, looking as big as ever.

"Hey, kid, how you doing?"

He didn't exactly push past me. But then again I didn't invite him. He just came in and went right to the living room.

I followed.

When I caught up to him he was standing there, staring at the tree.

"Nice tree," he said. He shifted his gaze slightly. "And you've put a stocking up. Got a little brother?"

I grinned sheepishly. "It's mine."

"Hey, it's Christmas."

"I guess."

Suddenly, he stopped. "What's that on top?"

"An angel."

"It looks . . . chewed."

"It was the rat. Remember, when I found him he was eating it. I showed you."

"Guess you did," Anje said. Then he turned to face me. "How'd it go last night?" he asked.

"Last night?"

"What you do, kid, sleep in? Or did you forget you were supposed to get out into the field last night, scouting around. Didn't you go?"

"Ah . . . yeah," I said, wondering why I lied.

His eyes hardened. "You sure?"

"Yes."

"Well, what did you see?"

"The . . . uh . . . rat."

"Find where he's hiding out?"

"Mr.—"

"Anje. Just Anje."

"Anje . . . I was thinking."

"Yeah, what?"

"I . . . ah . . . don't think I want to do this."

A moment of silence. "Don't want to *what?*"

"Kill the rat."

He didn't say anything. He just stared at me.

I said, "Is that . . . okay?"

"Wait a minute," he replied. "You saying you don't *want* that rat dead?" There was a snarl in his voice.

"No, I'm just saying . . . well . . . " I stared at my feet. "*I* don't want to do it."

"You did yesterday, dude."

"Well, I . . . just . . . don't want to . . . now."

"People," he murmured. Then he took a deep breath and said, "Okay. But just so you understand, I intend to do the job. It's who I am. Kind of a calling, if you know what I mean. I could always use some help, but hey, nobody's perfect. Only don't interfere. You hear me?"

I didn't know what to say.

"Do you?"

"Yeah."

"Sure?"

"Yeah."

"Okay."

Without another word, or even looking back at me, he went right to our hall, walked out, and slammed the door behind him.

Feeling sort of weak, as if I had done something wrong, I sat down. Then I reminded myself that it was Anje who was strange. I sighed, wishing the whole thing would just go away.

I called Cory. He no longer had a fever—that's what his sister said—but he was still in bed. We could probably get together after Christmas. "Cory would really like that," she said. "Merry Christmas, Eric."

By this time I was hating Merry Christmas.

In the living room I turned on the TV just in time to get an extra weather report. It was getting colder. A break was not expected until Christmas Day. I felt trapped. Like a rat.

-2-

I lay on the couch and watched some cartoons. When they became too boring, I picked up a book. Reading wasn't any better. I was too restless to concentrate.

I went into my parents' room and pulled out my main Christmas present from under their bed, the radio-controlled car. I unpacked it carefully, making sure I didn't break the cardboard box.

The Rebound 4 x 4 Jet Car was about ten inches long and had these four very large wheels, a red streamlined car body on the top, an equally streamlined blue truck—complete with cargo bay— on the bottom. There was also a control box with double toggle controls and a wire antenna. Having used Pete's model—the Turbo—lots of times, I knew how to work this one.

I slipped some batteries in—a red light came on to show they were good—set it on the ground, clicked the ON switch, and shifted the two toggles. Right off, the car zipped around the room, turning, flipping, spinning, shifting from one direction to another. Cool. It cheered me up.

Then I got bothered. After all, it was supposed to be my parents' Christmas gift to me. I repacked it carefully and put it back under the bed just the way it had been.

At eleven o'clock, I decided I would take the money Dad had given me and go to the arcade. If I played the games I knew well—like Rock Team Road Racer—I could string out the ten bucks for at least a couple of hours. I mean, it was something to do. I called my father's store and left him a message about where I was going.

Dressed for the cold, I got on the elevator and pushed the LOBBY button. The thing made its regular going-down noises. But suddenly I had to see what was going on down in the basement. Impulsively, I pushed the BASEMENT button.

Since I had pushed the LOBBY button first, it

stopped there. A guy was about to get on, but when I said, "I'm going down," he quickly said, "I'll wait," and backed out. It was as if the basement was a place to avoid. Or maybe it was me.

Though the lights were on, the place seemed empty. But as I walked around, I saw small white paper cups set against the walls. In each cup there were brown pellets. I picked up one of the cups to take a closer look. Sniffed it, too. It had a bitter smell. I was pretty sure it was poison, which meant Anje had been there. I put the cup down and hurried back to the elevator.

I kept thinking about Anje. His bright eyes, pale face, long blond hair. He reminded me of someone: I couldn't figure out who. But why did the guy care so much about killing one rat? The animal was probably only coming in from the cold. As soon as the freeze was over, I was sure the rat would go away.

I sort of guessed that none of that mattered to Anje. The guy wanted the rat dead. Hadn't he said he liked killing? The arcade, I reminded myself. Get the rat stuff out of your mind!

I went outside. Man, it was frigid.

I had gone about two blocks in the direction of the arcade when I came to a sudden stop. I was so upset I was almost crying. And I knew why. It was the whole exterminator-rat thing. The thought of Anje coming into our apartment building—probably using his own keys—to kill that rat really got to me.

Standing there on the freezing street I decided it wasn't just that I didn't like Anje, I didn't want that rat killed. After all, it *was* Christmas. . . . People were supposed to be happy, full of life and love. Know what I mean? But this . . . all of sudden I had to do something.

I wheeled around and, walking fast, I went back to the basement. I gathered up all the cups and dumped them—along with the poison pellets—into one of those ash cans.

Only then did I go to the arcade. I loved that place. Bright, flashing lights. Sounds of explosions, shots, crashes. Like being inside a cartoon action show. I was feeling so good I stretched out my ten bucks for two and half hours of play. Awesome!

Even better, in Time Crisis, I came in with one of highest scores, second only to Angel One.

A little after four that afternoon, I was home watching television, stretched out on the couch munching chips or something, when the phone rang.

"Hello?"

"Eric?"

"Yeah?"

"Anje. The exterminator. Hey, bud, you mess around with those poison cups?"

I sat up fast. "Well . . ."

"Did you?"

"What do you . . . mean?"

"I put down some poison cups in your basement. The Eden Apartments. Do I have that right? Did you touch them?"

"Well . . . yeah."

He didn't say anything. The silence went on for such a long time I wasn't sure he was still there.

But he was.

"Listen up, dude," he said, his voice hard. "Listen up *good*. I've got a job to do and I intend to do it. That rat is going to die. Don't interfere. Don't get in the way. Don't mess with me. You understand?"

"Yes, sir."

"I'm going down into the basement. I want you there."

I swallowed hard. "Why?"

"Be there!"

"Yes, sir."

Anje was waiting for me when I stepped out of the elevator.

He glared at me. His mustache made him look so fierce. It caught the light. "I just like to look a traitor in the eye," he said. "Now get out of here and let me do my work," he snapped. "And dude . . ."

I turned.

"Just so's you don't misunderstand, the only thing I hate more than rats is traitors."

I turned away.

"And another thing," he called.

I looked back.

"You made a deal."

"I did?"

"Think about it."

I retreated into the elevator. As the door slid shut, I could feel Anje's eyes on me. Man, I felt like crying. I was ashamed of myself. Only I was scared, too. And angry. All at once. I also felt I had to do *something*. But I didn't know what.

With a jab of my finger I punched the LOBBY button. When I got there I went to check the mailbox. We had some mail, but the only keys I had in my pocket were for the apartment and the storage bay. There was nothing I could do about it. But instead of going back up, I waited where I was.

When I heard the elevator open, and boots clumping away, I peeked around the corner. It was the exterminator leaving the building.

Soon as he was gone, I went back to the basement. Just as I had guessed, there were new cups. I scooped them up—along with the new poison pellets—and dumped them all into an ash can.

I was still angry, still scared, and pretty glad when I got back to our apartment. I double-bolted the door shut. But I had made up my mind. I didn't care what happened: I wasn't going to let that rat be killed.

-3-

"All this hanging around with nothing to do," my mother said to me. "I think you're getting depressed." She was smiling, trying to be kind. She and I were eating dinner alone because my father had to stay late at his store.

"Did you get out at all?" she asked.

"Went to the arcade."

"Have fun?"

"Yeah."

"Good! Just three more days," she said, smiling. "Crazy Christmas will be over."

"It's not just that," I said.

"Oh, what is it?"

"It's . . . there's no one to hang around with."

"No one?"

I explained the friend situation again.

"I'm sorry. Do you want to come to work with me tomorrow? You'll probably be bored there, too. But maybe not...."

"I'll be okay," I insisted. "But I was thinking, maybe I could get a model. Something to work on ... I have some money."

"Happy to help," she said, patting my hand. "Oh, we got some Christmas cards. From your father's Aunt Becky, and the Fosters. The church too, I guess, though it wasn't signed. But it's not the one they usually send."

After dinner I looked at the cards. The one from our church had a picture of the stained-glass window I liked, you know, Mary and the angel. The printed message inside read:

May the Message of Christmas Be with You!

At about eight there was a long-distance call from Aunt Thelma. Knowing that my mother would be talking for a long time, I grabbed the flashlight and slipped out of the apartment and went down to the basement.

It was dark, but there were no new cups.

At first I was puzzled. Maybe Anje had given up. That didn't seem like him. So I walked around looking for some clue about what he might have left instead. Sure enough, I found more pellets. They were hidden in odd, out-of-the-way places.

I gathered up as many as I could find—maybe fifty—and stuffed them into my pockets. I emptied them all into an ash can. But I didn't doubt he would bring more.

It occurred to me that there was no real garbage in the basement. I was pretty sure they incinerated everything. So I figured there was no food for the rat. My idea was, if I could leave some, maybe it would keep him from touching any of the poison I missed.

In the apartment, my mother was still on the phone.

I washed my hands, then collected some dinner scraps from the garbage pail, wrapped them in foil, and sneaked them back to the basement. I left the scraps near the place where I'd seen the rat digging a hole.

At the elevator, just before stepping into it, I called out, "Don't worry. I'll protect you!"

If I could keep the rat alive until Christmas I figured he'd be all right. The cold snap was supposed to lift. Then the rat could go away. It was only a matter of time. And holding off Anje.

As I slept that night I was disturbed briefly by the phone ringing. A glance at the clock by my bed told me it was two o'clock in the morning. When the ringing stopped I rolled over and slept, but not very well.

TWO DAYS BEFORE CHRISTMAS

I only woke when my father sat on my bed.

"Eric?"

"Yeah . . ."

"You up?"

My eyes were barely open. "I think so."

"Eric, I need to ask you something."

"What?"

"We got a call last night. Two o'clock in the morning."

I was awake now, knowing what was coming. "You did?"

"A man said he was the exterminator in the building. Said you were interfering with his work. I told him he had a wrong number. But he insisted it was you. Knew your name. He was pretty angry."

I stared at my father. "What did you say?"

"I told him he was nuts. The time and all. I told him to go away. That I would call the police."

"What did he say?"

"He hung up."

"Oh."

"Eric, do you know anything about this?"

I thought for a bit and then I said, "Well . . . remember the exterminator that came?"

"No."

"On Monday. Mom said he'd be coming."

"Oh, yeah," he said vaguely.

"Well . . . he wanted me to help him."

"Help him with what?"

"Ah . . . extermination."

"Hmmm. Not proper. Not at all."

"I told him . . . no," I lied.

"Good for you. That was the right answer. You have any idea what his name was?"

"Anje. Anjela Gabrail."

"You sure that's it?"

"Yeah. There's a card he gave me in my pants

pocket." I pointed to the clothes that I had flung over a chair.

My father found the card and held it up. In the dim room its redness looked like a blood spot. "I don't want you to have anything to do with this guy," he said to me. "I intend to call the company. I'll make sure he doesn't bother you."

"I'll be all right."

"I'm sure. But it's rather odd behavior. Two o'clock in the morning. Hey, but cheer up, fella. Only two more days to wait."

"I know."

"What are you going to do for fun today?"

"Mom said I could build a model."

"Great idea. Now get some more sleep. And make sure you don't let anyone in."

I rolled over and closed my eyes.

When I finally got up I found a twenty-dollar bill on the kitchen table. "**Get a difficult model**," the message read. My dad's handwriting.

I was surprised by the amount. It meant that he was worried about me.

After breakfast I turned on my computer and

checked the local weather on the Internet. Not too good. A frigid Canadian air mass had simply stalled over our region. No letup in the cold. But relief would be on the way by Friday.

As I was using the computer, there was a beep, which meant I had some E-mail.

There was a message. It read:

> **Eric,**
> **Don't mess with me!**
> **Anje**

I noticed his address. It was Deadrats@TMI.org. I deleted it fast then called Pete's, hoping his mother would be there. She wasn't, but this time their machine worked. I left a message, asking for his phone number in Florida.

I dressed for the cold, but before I went out I checked the basement. In the place where I had left the food, only a few crumbs remained. No foil either. Did that mean the rat had eaten it all, or had Anje taken it away? I didn't know.

I went outside.

Guess what? The cold was worse. I know that's what the weather people had said, but I hadn't really believed it. This was definitely worse than yesterday. People had scarfs around their noses and mouths. Walking fast. When they breathed it looked as if they were on fire. I tried running but it was hard with all the ice on the sidewalks.

The model store was part of a small shopping strip a few blocks from our street. I hadn't been in for a while, what with school and all. I thought about what I wanted to build. A car model? A plane? Maybe some fantasy or sci-fi thing. As long as it took a lot of time to make, I didn't really care. I wanted to keep busy, keep my mind off you-know-what.

When I reached the shop I stopped to look in the display window. Airplanes and rockets dangled in the air. A squadron of X-Wing Fighters seemed to be in a dogfight with multicolored World War I tri- and biplanes. On the bottom, an electric train went round and round a small oval of track. Tanks, armored vehicles, farm tractors, and sports cars were arranged here and there. Army figures and fantasy figures were ready to attack.

In the center of the railway oval was a Christmas scene. You know: Mary and Joseph, and baby Jesus, along with the three kings and an angel who looked sort of like the stained-glass angel in our church. It was weird the way he kept popping up.

Around the infant Jesus were lots of animals and shepherds.

I studied the scene closely, but I didn't see a rat among the animals. Maybe rats weren't invited. Too ugly. And here I was, trying to save one. Too much.

To my surprise there were no customers in the store. I figured it was the cold. Behind a counter this guy was reading a magazine. He looked up, nodded to me, went back to his reading. For just a second I freaked. I mean, I thought he was Anje. But, of course, it wasn't. Couldn't be.

Anyway, the shelves were stuffed with boxes of models. There were racks of glue, paints, knives, and model magazines.

I walked around, looking at the pictures on the boxes, trying to decide what I wanted. It was hard to make up my mind.

The guy behind the counter looked up again. "How much you got to spend, dude?" he asked.

"Twenty and change."

"That section over there," he said, pointing toward the back of the store. "All twenty and under."

I went where he told me and looked over the boxes, wondering if there was something I could get that would help protect the rat. You know, like a tank that really worked.

Then I saw these bags of plastic soldiers. They were dark green, maybe two inches tall. Each soldier was shooting a rifle. The bags had forty soldiers each and were only a dollar a bag. Made in China.

I did some quick figuring. Twenty bucks, twenty bags, times forty. Eight hundred soldiers! Totally awesome!

I bought them. The man behind the counter said, "War gamer, dude?"

"Sort of," I said.

"Merry Christmas."

"Merry Christmas."

I hurried back home, grabbed the white flashlight and went down to the basement. The lights were off. When I got to the place where I had seen the rat, I ripped open the bags and dumped the soldiers out. What I did was put the soldiers around the hole, guns pointing out. Like, see, they were defending the rat hole. It wasn't easy. Sometimes I knocked one down, which sent others over. Anyway, it took more than two hours to set the eight hundred up. A regular army. Awesome.

Of course, I knew perfectly well that there was no way in the world these plastic soldiers would help the rat, or hold back Anje. But, you know, I just wanted it to say, like, the rat wanted to be alive. I mean, Anje was in the army. He might get the point.

Up in the apartment I got some bread slices, then took them back with me and left them right by the hole. I figured my army wasn't just protecting the rat, but the food supply too.

Okay. I had done something.

When I got upstairs I just barely made it to the ringing phone.

It was my father. "Eric," he said, "I checked

with the apartment management people. They said they never heard of this Mr. Gabrail. He doesn't work for them."

My heart sank. "Dad, remember? I showed you his card?"

"I know you did."

"And Dad, he has these keys that fit the whole building."

"Look, Eric, I do believe you. But if you're concerned—I am—simply double-lock the door from inside. And don't let anyone in. Can you do that?"

"Yeah." I'd already been doing that. "Sure."

"I mean it. It'll be impossible to get in."

"I know."

"Hey, cheer up. Christmas Eve tomorrow."

"Don't worry, we'll win," I replied glumly.

"Win what?" father asked.

"Ah . . . never mind."

ONE DAY BEFORE CHRISTMAS

-1-

I *woke in the* middle of the night.

I'm sure I hadn't heard anything. I mean, I'm a pretty good sleeper. Used to be, anyway. All the same, I had this feeling that something was happening in the basement. So I rolled over and looked at the alarm clock and saw that it was a little past two in the morning. Anje's favorite time.

I lay back, sort of, you know, edgy, pulled the blankets up to my chin, and just stared up at the dark ceiling. I heard a few cars passing outside and, for a brief, annoying time, a car alarm. There was wind too, a soft moaning right outside my window. The more I lay there the more I wanted to know about my army.

I slipped out of bed. There was some light coming from somewhere and it took me a moment to realize it was the little flashlight Anje had given me. It was glowing again, giving enough light for me to find my shirt and trousers. I didn't bother with shoes, just stepped into my slippers. I did make sure I had keys and I took the flashlight, too.

Quietly, I unbolted the door locks, checked to see if anyone was in the hallway. No one. Then I slipped out, pulled the door shut, and buzzed for the elevator. It clanked up and opened. I got on and was just about to push the button for the basement when I stopped. There was this faint scent of poison gas. Anje's smell. Did that mean he had just been on the elevator?

I hesitated. That elevator was noisy. If Anje was in the basement, he'd hear me coming for sure. I decided it might be better to walk. So I pushed the button for the lobby. The elevator started down, groaning and grinding as usual. Nervous, I almost pushed the STOP button, but held back.

The lobby was cold. At this time of night the heat was turned off. There was some snow tracked from the front door to right where I stood by the elevator. But I didn't see anyone.

Moving softly, I went to the back of the lobby and opened the stairwell door. The only light came from a glowing red EXIT sign shining downwards.

I stopped and asked myself: Do I really want to do this?

There was enough *yes* to keep going.

Grasping the banister—it was like an icicle—I started down the steps. They circled around four times before reaching the bottom landing.

Heart pounding, I eased the door open a crack and leaned forward.

The place was pitch black.

I flicked on my flashlight and poked the beam right and left. Nothing. I turned it off, and put it in my pocket. It still glowed.

I opened the door further, wide enough to stick

my head in and look around. There was no light or sound. Maybe, I thought, nothing was happening.

Feeling braver, I took a step, letting the door shut behind me with a soft *clunk*.

I stood still and waited for my heart rate to get down to normal. All the while I stared into the dark and listened hard. I was hoping my eyes would adjust to the blackness but there was no adjustment to make. I decided the flashlight glow might give me away, so I left it by the door. That way, at least, I could find my way out.

I stepped away from the stairwell. Around one turn. Pretty soon the blackness was complete. I would have to feel my way.

As I remembered it, the stairwell was pretty much opposite where I wanted to go.

Hands before me, taking small steps, I started forward, trying to make no sound at all. Unexpectedly I touched something hard. Wiggling my fingers I reached out again and felt this clammy flatness. It was a concrete wall.

Hands pressed against it, I moved along to the right until I smashed into something metallic.

I mean, the sound exploded. It was so loud I jumped—as if I hadn't made the sound—myself.

Gulping air, I was afraid to move. If Anje was down there, no way he didn't hear that sound. And if he did hear he'd know it was me.

Trying not to panic, I clenched my fists and took a deep breath, letting the air out slowly.

I realized I had walked into the row of ash cans. Fine. That meant the elevator was behind me. If I'd remembered it right, the direction I wanted to take was straight ahead.

I stared into the darkness, ears straining. I had no sense that anything else alive was there.

Nervous, I inched forward, having been in the basement enough times now to be pretty sure of the way. So I was startled when I came around the third turn and saw some light ahead. It was low, flickering. Like, you know, something was burning. There was this stink too.

Clinging to the wall with two hands, I crept forward. The light grew brighter. It was just around a corner. I moved my head so I could peek out with one eye.

There was Anje. He was sitting cross-legged on the cement floor, with what was left of my plastic army in front of him. Next to him was this ash can. Licks of fire rose up out of it.

As I watched, Anje plucked up one of my toy soldiers. Grasping it with both hands, he twisted it until, with a snap, he broke the figure in two. Then he tossed the pieces into the can, where I guess they burned or at least melted.

I watched, scared but fascinated too.

He reached for another soldier and repeated the same weird moves.

After he had burned up the whole army, he hitched himself forward, waved flames and smoke away with a hand, and peered into the can.

He must have been satisfied with what he saw. He stood, lifted the can and tipped it over, pouring what I think was hot, liquid plastic into the rat hole.

Gagging, I clapped a hand over my mouth to keep from throwing up. Then I backed away as fast as I could without making a sound. When I reached a place I thought was halfway to the steps,

I stopped. Hoping to get my breath back, I pressed my forehead against the cool wall. It helped calm me down.

At last I looked up. I suppose there were still some flames because there was reddish light casting shadows on the walls.

All of sudden there was this banging sound, as if an ash can had been struck. Then I heard Anje's voice shouting, "There you are!"

Next moment, from around the corner, I saw the rat coming. He was racing right toward me. In nothing flat he passed to my left.

More scared of Anje than the rat, I ran too. In fact I followed the rat, only to smash right into a wall. Stunned, hurting, I turned and ran again, stumbling and crashing into what I think was a can. Anyway, I fell. But I forced myself up and crawled behind the can, then hunkered down as tightly as I could.

Moments later I saw a beam of light moving about. It came from Anje's long black flashlight. With my heart pounding, I held my breath.

He walked right by me. Couldn't have been

more than four feet away. Then he was gone. I wasn't sure where he was going until I heard the elevator clanking down, the doors opening and shutting, and finally the sounds of the thing going up.

Letting out a sigh of relief, I stood up and made my way to the elevator. It had stopped moving. I was just about to push the button when I held back. Maybe Anje was on it. Maybe this was a trap.

Afraid to take the chance, I went to the stairwell door. The white flashlight was where I'd left it, still glowing. If he had seen it, he'd have known I was down there.

For the first time I had this thought: the flashlight, the one he'd given me with his name on the side, maybe he gave it to me for some reason. I mean, a reason other than the one he said, which was so I could see. Maybe—and it made me cold to think it—maybe, he gave it to me so *he* could always see *me*.

All the same, I picked it up and climbed the six floors to our apartment.

Soon as I got into my bed, I drew the blankets over my head and just hugged myself. I was feeling exhausted. Not that I could sleep.

I was thinking too much.

As far as I could tell the rat was safe. Okay. That was good. I was really glad about that. But there was still one more day before the cold eased off. See, my hope was still that when it got warmer, the rat would leave the building. So the final test would come tomorrow.

No! Later today.

-2-

It was almost eleven o'clock before I woke up again. It was still Thursday, the day before Christmas. Later, Christmas Eve. My first thought was, What's happened in the basement?

I stumbled into the kitchen where I found a note.

> *Christmas Eve is almost here!*
> *We should be home no later than seven.*
> *Special dinner. Stay warm!*
> *Love you,*
> *Mom*

I dressed, and was just about to head out for the elevator when the phone rang.

Thinking it might be one of my parents checking in, I rushed back inside and snatched up the phone.

"Hello?"

"Good try, kid," came Anje's hard voice. "You surprised me. You really did. Too bad those soldiers weren't real. But hey, one night left for the mission. I'm hyped. Hope you are. Now, I'm willing to make a deal with you. Whoever is alive in the morning gets to stay alive. How's that for a Christmas present? We got a deal?"

"I . . . guess," I said, not knowing what else to say.

"May the best rat win. And don't forget, I think you're a rat, too."

"What do you mean?"

"Hey, you didn't forget did you?"

"What?"

"Come on, dude. You swore you'd attack all rats in your vicinity, or pay the penalty."

"I did?"

"Yeah. Merry Christmas," he added. Then there was nothing but a dial tone.

Shook up, I put the phone down slowly and went back to my room. What was the guy saying? Was I the Christmas rat? It sure sounded like it.

I picked up the little flashlight. Glowing again. I stood there, I don't know for how long, trying to decide whether to take it with me or not. I mean, what if it really was his way of finding me?

In the end I decided I'd take it, but I made up my mind to leave it down there.

Out in the hallway I called up the elevator. When it reached my floor our old lady neighbor, Miss Cromwell, stepped out.

"Merry Christmas, Eric!" she said as she went by.

"Oh, yeah, Merry Christmas, Miss Cromwell," I mumbled.

She went on down the hall.

"Miss Cromwell!" I called.

She stopped and turned. "Yes, Eric?"

"Ah . . . the other day, did any exterminator come to your place?"

Miss Cromwell thought for a moment, then

shook her head. "No, I don't think so. Did I miss him? They usually come in the spring. Do you need one?"

"No. Just asking," I said.

"Oh. Bye now," she said. "Have a lovely day tomorrow."

"Bye . . ." I said, watching her go.

What is going on? I asked myself, feeling totally creeped out. I mean, I was positive I'd seen Anje go to her place on Monday. *Positive.*

But had I seen him go *in?* I tried to imagine that moment. No, I hadn't actually *seen* him do it. Was I imagining everything?

I looked at the glowing white flashlight in my hand. No way was this all in my head.

I turned back to the elevator, but I heard the phone ring in our apartment. I rushed inside.

"Hey, man, how you doing?" It was Pete. It was so good to hear his voice.

"Hey, you back?" I said, hopefully.

"Nope. Still down in warm, sunny Florida. Ma said you called. Said it's frozen up there."

"Totally."

"Hey, what's happening?"

I wanted to tell him about Anje. But I felt weird. I mean, there was something not right. Maybe I *was* imagining the whole thing. You know, a dream, the way they do sometimes in dumb movies and books.

"Nothing much," I said to him.

"Well, I just wanted to say hi. Can't talk long. Be back on Monday. Let's hang out."

"I'm . . . pretty sure I'm getting a radio-controlled car."

"Cool! See ya."

"See ya."

I studied the phone for a moment. Then, wanting to prove something, I went out into the hallway. For a moment I just stood there, not sure what I was doing. I stared out the hall window looking for I don't know what. Finally I got on the elevator and, holding the door open, sniffed. No Anje smell. I went down. When I stepped into the basement all was calm, all was bright— lights on—just like in the Christmas hymn. I mean, other than the faint smell of burnt plastic, everything seemed pretty much the way it was supposed to be.

I went down along the corridors, passing the ash cans and the storage bays until I reached where the rat had been digging. Or what was left. Now it was capped with a bulging bubble of green plastic.

Kneeling, I poked at it with a finger. It was rock hard. Hey, no way was *that* my imagination. These things were happening. To me, anyway.

I thought about the rat. He had escaped, which was good. I did wonder where he'd gone. I mean, now I really wanted to protect him. Felt I had to, until Christmas morning, anyway.

As I stood there the idea came to me that if I left the door to the stairwell open, maybe the rat could get out that way. Then I realized that between the basement and the doors to the street he'd have to go through the lobby doors, too. No way they could all be left open. Not in this cold.

Discouraged, I sat on the floor with my back against the wall, closed my eyes, and tried to decide on a plan. If only I could get the rat past Christmas—if I could trust Anje—he'd stay alive. But how? There was nothing to do, I told myself, feeling hopeless and angry.

As I sat there I wondered why I cared so much about the dumb rat. After a while I decided it wasn't the rat, really, it was the exterminator. Right. I cared about Anje because he was scary. What was he trying to do to me? I mean, who *was* he?

Disappointed in myself for not being able to think of answers or any plan about saving the rat, I walked back toward the elevator, stopping in front of the storage bays. Which was ours? Thirteen?

I counted out the bays. Thirteen was the next to the last. I peered through the steel mesh. Yep. I recognized Dad's numbering system.

As I gazed at it, I had this idea that if I could lure the rat into the bay, and lock him in—the mesh was fine enough to hold him—I might keep him safe. Then I remembered that he had gotten in on his own. I mean, he had been chewing that angel. So maybe he could get out. But if there was a hole somewhere maybe I could plug it. Anyway, I figured my idea was at least worth a try. I decided to explore the possibilities.

I reached into my pocket and, sure enough, there was the key to the storage bin. I had never put it back in the drawer.

I unlocked the door and swung it open, then started moving boxes around to see if there was a hole the rat had used.

I found it pretty quick.

It was in the back wall, near the floor. I mean, I couldn't be sure it was the way he got in, but it was the only way I could figure it. Anyway, I opened one of the boxes, poked around, and found this small metal cup. Maybe it was my first drinking cup. It was pretty dinky. But guess what? I shoved the small end into the hole—and it fit. Then, with my fist, I sort of pounded it. Like putting a cork back into a bottle.

Now, the bay would hold the rat but how could I lead him into it? Maybe if I left a food trail or . . . *the radio-controlled car!* Awesome! A totally cool idea.

But . . . wouldn't Anje be able to open the bay door with his keys? Not if I broke our key off in the lock. No way.

Excited, I hurried back to the apartment and

pulled my parents' gift out from under their bed. Like the first time, I unpacked it very carefully. Then I found some cheese in the fridge. I took everything back to the basement.

Now I had no clue where the rat might be, so I set the car on the floor—cargo side up. I tore the cheese into bits and loaded them on. With everything ready, I flicked the switch. The battery light flickered, then turned bright, just like with Pete's. Then I stepped back and moved the toggle switches. The car sped off, much too fast. I adjusted the toggles so that it moved at a slow crawl.

Making sure the bay door was open, I stayed as far behind the car as possible while keeping it in sight, driving it along the corridors to the place where the rat had its hole, the one Anje had sealed up. There, I spun the car around—one toggle forward, one back—so that it faced away toward #13. Then I turned everything off. The whole idea was this: If the rat was somewhere close it would smell the cheese and come out, then follow the car—which I'd control down the corridor and into the bay. I loved it.

Ready to wait a good while, I turned off the

basement lights. Using Anje's flashlight, I found my way back to where I'd put my army, then sat cross-legged on the ground. The toggle box was in my lap, the flashlight beam pointing forward, my eyes fairly well glued to the car.

I'm not sure how long I waited. I might have dozed. I mean, I hadn't slept so great the night before. But all of a sudden the rat was there, sniffing around the cheese in the back of the car. I could see his nose wiggle as he drew closer to the food.

Startled, I almost dropped the toggle box. Good thing I checked myself. I needed to act carefully.

So I waited. As I did, I saw the rat rise up on his hind legs, paws on the car, sort of investigating. He leaned further forward. There it was: He was nibbling the cheese.

Very gently, I moved the toggle bars forward. With a jerk, the car began to roll. Startled, the rat jumped back, edged away, then sort of looked over his shoulder at the car. Like he was unsure of himself.

I stopped the car.

The rat eyed it, took one step then another few

steps toward it. I waited until he climbed into the car again and began to nibble. I moved the toggle bars again. The car moved. As before, the rat backed off. But not so far as he did the first time.

Slowly, steadily I kept the car moving. The rat, his tail switching, followed right down the corridor. Almost made me laugh.

As the car moved toward me, I stood up and pressed myself against the wall. The rat kept following the car—except he did stop when he went past me, lifting his snout and sniffing the air, as if checking me out. I didn't seem to bother him because he continued on.

Soon as he moved beyond me, I got up and began to follow.

When the car reached our storage bay, I stopped it, and let the rat take another bite of the cheese. Then, really carefully, I moved one toggle switch, turning the car ninety degrees. It was now facing the open bay door.

Okay. I aimed the car right into the bay. It was almost there when it stopped. Dead. I looked down at my control box just in time to see the red battery light fade and die. The batteries had given out. Dang!

Next thing I heard was the elevator descending. Someone was coming.

Panicking, I dropped the toggle box, started for the bay, stopped and instead raced away along the corridor, took a corner, and halted.

I could hear the elevator doors open. Then footsteps. Afraid to look, afraid not to, I peeked out from the corner.

It was Anje. He was shining his long black flashlight.

I retreated further into the basement, then stopped and listened. More footsteps, finally silence. Then I heard something different. A *twang!*

Right away I knew what it was. He was using his crossbow. Next minute I heard the slam of a door. The steps grew louder, then softer. After that came the sound of the elevator going up. Then nothing but silence.

I don't know how long I held still to be sure things were safe. Quite a while, I think. At last, I crept from my hiding place. Heart pounding, I made my way back to the bay wall. When I reached #13 I saw that the bay door was shut and locked. The radio-controlled car was nowhere in sight. The toggle box was gone, too.

Anje had taken them.

Just to realize what he'd done, what he *knew,* made me feel sick to my stomach. How was I going to explain things to my parents? Right off, I thought I could say he'd come into the apartment and stolen it. But, aside from the fact that it wasn't true, it would mean more lies.

I went back to the apartment. What was I going to do? My parents would be so freaked.

I checked the time. 2:00 P.M. There wasn't much choice. From my bottom drawer I took out all the money I had saved. Something like fifty bucks. I threw on my coat, then hurried to a toy store that carried the cars. The place was mobbed. You know, Christmas Eve. How could people wait so long to get with it?

Anyway, I went to the shelves where the radio-controlled cars were. They had them all right, but the model my folks had gotten me was sold out. The only one left was the model I had wanted.

I had the money, but now I couldn't get the better one. They might notice, and how was I going to explain that?

Really upset, I went up to the sales counter. There were a couple of people working there.

"Excuse me, please. I'm really looking for one of those radio-controlled four-by-four models. Not the Turbo. The other one."

The sales clerk gave me a sad smile. "Sorry. All gone. Really popular model. Just the more expensive ones left."

I stood there, not knowing what to do.

Then this other clerk looked up. "Hold on. Some big blond guy just returned one. He said it had been used only twice. Doesn't have the packing, though. So I could give it to you with a discount. Ten percent off. Want it?"

I looked at him stupidly, trying to take in what he had said.

"Do you?" he asked again.

If I bought back that one—and it must have been the same one I had—I wouldn't be able to get the better model I wanted. But at least my parents would be okay.

"Yeah," I said.

The clerk got the car. I handed over my money. Back in the apartment, I got it into its original box.

I slumped onto my bed, feeling relieved, trying to understand what had happened. Then, all of a sudden, I remembered the rat. I'd been so freaked about the car, I had forgotten all about him. And I had heard the crossbow.

Really upset—mostly at myself—I tore down to the basement and, using the white flashlight, looked around. I didn't see any sign of the rat. Did that mean he was dead? I made my way back to the corridor. I waited and listened.

After twenty minutes I heard a squeak. My heart jumped. The rat was alive. I can't tell you how glad I was. Then and there I made a sort of vow that I wouldn't forget him again. Not in the few hours left.

In our living room, I sat down on the couch. I was just waiting for what I knew what would happen next.

Sure enough, the phone rang.

It was Anje.

"Got to hand it to you, dude. You keep trying. But guess what? Christmas is coming and you're going to lose."

He hung up.

I went into the living room and checked the weather on TV. Though it was still very cold, for the first time there they were saying it would warm up for Christmas day. "Ordinarily," the announcer chirped gaily, "we'd be wishing you a white Christmas. But this year, a *warmer* Christmas will be the gift everyone desires. In the meantime, stay cozy and keep indoors!"

I sighed. If I could protect the rat for eight more hours I was sure—somehow—he would go off on his own. See, I couldn't get it out of my head that just getting to Christmas would solve everything.

The only problem was, I felt tired and full of

tears. I was scared about what Anje might do. I mean, I was pretty sure he was after me now as much as the rat.

Anyway, I took up his little flashlight and went down to the basement. The lights were on. I turned them off. Then I made my way to the place where the rat had been, where he had dug his hole. And what I did was place the flashlight—which was glowing and all—next to the hole. I turned off the beam. The glowing gave enough light.

Then I just sat down, back against the wall. The way I figured it, if Anje came he might as well find me near where the rat was. Because, guess what? The way I saw it, it was me and the rat . . . against Anje.

Actually I don't know how long I sat there, thinking thoughts, probably dozing now and again. But once, when I woke up, I saw the rat. Only he was curled up next to the flashlight, sides heaving slightly. He was as fast asleep as I'd been.

I gazed at him. And I remembered how scared I was when I first saw him. Sure, he had surprised me. And he was ugly too. Those beady eyes, chisel teeth, naked tail.

Except now he looked—not exactly beautiful—but, you know, sort of *not* scary.

As I watched him he stirred, lifted his head, opened his eyes. He seemed to be looking at me the way I was looking at him. Maybe he was remembering how, that first time, I had scared *him*. Anyway, he lowered his head, curled up, and went to sleep again.

Anje didn't show.

I could hear myself thinking that maybe he wouldn't come. But you know, I didn't really believe it.

After a while I picked up the flashlight—the rat didn't even stir—and went back to the elevator. Just before I stepped in I decided to get rid of the flashlight. It was too creepy. I put it on the floor, glowing. But once I had, I stood there, watching it. I must have been very quiet, because, like out of nowhere, the rat appeared. He was sniffing around the flashlight. As I watched, amazed, he first put his front paws up on it. Then he began to roll it away. Made me remember how Anje said rats took stuff.

As I watched him go down the corridor—the soft light slowly vanishing—I had a thought that made me smile. The rat was taking Anje's flashlight. My Christmas gift to the rat. After all, it was Christmas Eve.

I don't think I ever wanted Christmas to come so badly. I mean, waiting for gifts is one thing. Wanting to see if you'd be alive is something else.

-4-

My father brought home a pizza with all the fixings for dinner. That and this really special Dutch chocolate he sells. My mother got us a huge box of Christmas cookies. We ate dinner at the kitchen table and talked about other Christmas Eves. Like we always did. They told some of the same stories about when they were kids too.

After dinner, with the CD of Christmas carols filling the apartment, Mom put out wrapping paper, tape, ribbon, cards, all that stuff. This was the time we wrapped gifts. We went into our own rooms for an hour or so. I was pretty sure they wouldn't notice that there was a whole new radio car, from me, for me, under their bed.

Next, as always, my mother made hot and spicy apple cider and served up the cookies. We sat on the couch and, by the twinkling tree lights, watched a video of *A Christmas Carol*. The old black-and-white British one. I'd seen it so often I could have said the lines before the actors spoke them, did, too. I always liked the ghosty parts best. The spirits and stuff.

It was supposed to be a warm, cozy evening. My parents were happy. They sure tried hard to get me into the groove. But the whole time I sort of felt outside of things. My mind was on the basement, the rat, Anje. I wasn't going to lose. Not if I could help it, though I felt helpless.

"It's been a hard week for you, hasn't it?" my dad said to me.

"All that doing nothing," Mom agreed.

"I guess so," I said, wishing I could share with them all that had happened. By this time I was afraid to.

"Well," my mother said cheerfully, "tomorrow it's finally supposed to warm up. Dinner at the Willobys'." Christmas at the Willobys'—old friends of my parents—was another tradition.

I brought out my gifts for my parents and put them under the tree. As always they would do theirs later after I had gone to bed. After kisses and hugs I went to my room. Must have been about ten o'clock. Had Anje already come? Had he found the rat? Had the flashlight given him away?

I couldn't sleep. But then, I didn't have any intention of doing so. Just to be sure, I set the alarm for 11:45. "What'll I do?" I asked myself. I didn't know. *Something.* I lay quietly in bed, not moving, listening to the sound of my parents as they brought out their presents and placed them about the tree. Since I already knew their other gifts for me, I found myself wondering what they would put in my stocking.

They went back into their room. The apartment grew quiet. After a while I got up and wandered out to the living room. The tree lights were twinkling. The gifts were all there. My Christmas stocking, hanging from the back of a chair, was bulging. This time I wouldn't look. I wanted it to be a surprise.

Feeling frustrated, I went back to bed and lay there, wide awake. The words to "Hark, the Herald Angels Sing" kept going through my head. I was feeling sick. It was the worst Christmas Eve of my life.

-5-

I woke with a start. I mean, I sat straight up in my bed, heart beating very fast. Someone was walking through the apartment. One of my parents? Was that the front door closing? Upset, I slipped out of bed, found my slippers and my clothes where I had left them on the floor.

I checked the clock. It was almost midnight! The alarm hadn't rung.

I crept into the living room, gazed out the window. The street below was deserted and still looked dead cold. I looked around at the tree and the presents. Then I realized my Christmas stocking was gone. It made me gasp. I couldn't even believe it. Maybe my parents had moved it. But I doubted it. I mean, it wasn't anywhere.

Was it Anje I heard walking around our apartment? Had he come in and taken the stocking? What was he going to do with it? Or was taking it meant to be bait—for me?

It might have been. But there was no way I could stay put. I figured I'd go crazy. I had to know what was happening.

I walked down the whole six floors. When I reached the basement door, I cracked it open a little and peeked in. The lights were off.

Holding my breath, I eased the door wide enough to let me squeeze through the gap. Then I closed it behind me very slowly, making sure it didn't click.

I breathed deeply and listened. I couldn't see or hear, but there didn't seem to be anything unusual happening.

I began to wish I had kept Anje's flashlight. But suddenly a really scary thought filled me. That glowing. Maybe the glow—I don't know how—had been protecting me. I didn't know how it worked, any more than I knew what Anje was all about. But, as long as I had it, things had been, like, okay for me. Well, sort of. Only I'd given the flashlight to the rat. Now, he was safe, maybe—and I wasn't.

So I stood there, trying to decide what to do. Maybe, I thought, I could get the flashlight back. I tried to remember where the rat had been heading.

Moving from the door, I started making my way down the corridor, hands before me.

I couldn't see of course, but by then I had a good sense of where things were. The further I went the more I knew that flashlight was gone.

But then I had another idea. Why shouldn't I turn on the basement lights? You know, to make myself feel safer. And the lights would keep the rat in his hiding place. I had nothing to hide. This building was where I lived.

Standing there, I tried to figure out where I was. If the basement door was back there, the electrical room was ... here.

I moved in that direction. My foot touched something hard. I reached out. It was a wall. When I felt around I touched a door. My heart leaped. Had I found the electrical door so easily? Fingers extended, I groped for a door handle. And found it. Twisting it, I pulled. The other times it had opened. This time it wouldn't.

Had Anje locked it? Did that mean he was expecting me? Waiting for me in the dark?

I turned away from the door, but didn't go far. Maybe, I told myself, I should just get out of there. Why should I care what happened to a rat? Just because it was alive? Big deal. What about me? Didn't I want to be alive? I kept telling myself, You're stupid, you're stupid.

Now I knew that right across the way from the electrical door was the elevator. What did I care if I was heard? I just needed to get back there, call the elevator down, and be free.

I took four steps across the floor and, if my hands hadn't been in front of me, I would have smashed right into the wall.

I felt about. There was a door. It had to be the

elevator door. I fumbled for the button. That would be by the side. Cool. I found it fast and pushed it. Except . . . nothing happened.

I pushed it again. A few times. There was no sound from the elevator. I didn't know how he did it, but I was sure as anything that Anje had turned it off. The way I once did to my folks.

Now I was fairly screaming to myself: *Get out of here!* I turned around, moving fast. Too fast. I tripped on my own feet, started to fall, twisted and righted myself. Stood straight.

When I was steady I realized I had turned around so much I no longer knew which direction I was facing. Was the stairwell in this direction . . . or that?

I reached my arms out to full length—fingers extended. No matter which way I turned, there was nothing but empty air.

There I was, in the basement of my own house—The Eden Apartments—totally lost.

Breathing deeply, clenching my fists now, I struggled to keep from getting into a total panic. "Be cool," I whispered to myself softly. "Be really cool." The sound of my own voice helped. I tried to center myself. Gradually, I got control.

Find a wall, I told myself, *and move along it. Move until you find something you know.*

Taking little steps, I followed my own orders.

I came up against a wall. Once there, I paused and rested and tried to determine where I was by moving my hands about. There was nothing but hard cement. I kept moving. I touched something. The door that led to the steps? No! Another wall. Walls all around me. I couldn't find the door. . . .

He had trapped me.

I felt so shaky, I thought I might fall. I turned, and found the elevator door. I leaned against it. I could just stay here, I told myself. Until morning. Until Christmas.

That was when I heard a sound.

It came from . . . I had no idea where. It was so small, so quick, I couldn't grasp what it was. I strained my ears. I hoped it would come again even as I wished it wouldn't.

It did. I knew what it was then: a squeak. The rat. He was still alive, moving about. I felt a surge of joy that almost made me laugh it was so stupid. How could I possibly care so much about a dumb, ugly rat?

No sooner did I ask myself than I heard another sound. It was a *click*. I knew what *that* was, too: the sound of Anje's crossbow being cocked.

I mean, he was standing in the dark somewhere with his crossbow cocked and ready to shoot. It came to me that in that darkness, if *I* made a sound, he might think *I* was the rat. Or was it me—all along—he was after?

Oh man, I felt cold, a lot colder than when I had been outside. I mean, didn't he say he thought of me like a rat? And then there was that penalty he said I'd agreed to. Yeah, he was going to shoot me.

And right about then I knew why I cared so much about the rat. Because he was alive. Just as I was alive. I wanted him to live. I wanted to live. I mean, it was Christmas.

Do something to stay alive, Eric! I fairly screamed at myself.

"It's me!" I shouted out loud. "Me! Eric. Eric Andrick. I'm over here!"

No answer.

"I know you're there Anje. I know you are!"

Again, no answer.

"Can't you say anything?" I screamed. "Come on!"

That time there was an answer from the dark. "I warned you about interfering, dude," came Anje's voice.

My knees nearly buckled, my stomach churned. "I'm sorry," I cried out. "I just want to go home. Please! Will you let me?"

"Go ahead and try," he replied.

"Why don't you let me go?" I asked.

"Because of what you did."

"What did I do?"

"You wanted to kill the rat."

"It was you who wanted to, not me!" I screamed.

"Just a test," he said. "Remember what you said? 'I got nothing better to do.' So you kill."

"But I changed my mind!"

"Too late, bud. You're the Christmas rat now. How does it feel to be the hunted one? To have someone after you? Makes you scream to be alive, doesn't it? Or is being alive," he sneered, "too *boring?*"

Fighting back tears, I knew I couldn't stay where I was, but I could only inch along the wall, hands pressed back against the cement.

My fingers came up against something. I stopped, felt around. It was a doorknob. The door to the steps. I was almost out of there. I gave the handle a twist. This time it moved. It gave a squeak.

The next second I heard a twanging sound, followed almost instantly by a spike of pain in my left leg. I screamed, twisted around, and stayed on my feet only because I was holding onto the doorknob. Then I pushed against it. The door opened. I dove forward toward the steps just as another crossbow bolt whizzed past me.

From the floor I swung, and, using my feet, kicked the door shut. Then, on all fours, I scrambled up the steps.

I reached the first floor. Gulping for air, I stopped and listened. I could hear the elevator. It was moving up. It was Anje—following me like some kind of stalker.

I headed up the steps, running all the way. Maybe I could beat him.

By the time I reached the second-floor landing I knew Anje would get there first. He'd be waiting for me on the fifth floor. I looked down. Blood was dripping into my slipper.

I made myself sit on the steps, next to the door marked SECOND FLOOR. I rolled up my pant leg and looked at my wound. The crossbow bolt had grazed my calf. It was cut all right, but I could see for myself it was mostly just bleeding.

I tried to think. Maybe, I thought, I'd be safest staying where I was.

I listened. I could hear nothing.

Using the banister as support I pulled myself up and opened the door a crack. From what I could see, the hallway was deserted. No sound of the elevator.

I let the door close and made my way up to the third floor. There I did as before: opened the door and peeked out. Again there was nothing.

The same on the fourth floor.

And the fifth. My floor. When I reached it, I was afraid to look out. Still, I knew what I had to do. Cautiously, using my fingertips, I pried open the door a little.

I could see nothing, but there was a rush of air. I noticed that the hall window was open.

Did that mean that Anje had left *that* way? Or was this some kind of trick he was playing? I sure didn't hear the elevator. Maybe he was still in it, waiting for me to go by.

My heart thudding, I opened the door further. Wherever he was, no one was in the hall. I pulled the door key from my pocket.

Taking a deep breath, I jumped out into the hall and ran as fast as I had ever run. Reaching our door, I slipped the key into the lock, got the door open, and squeezed inside.

It took me less than two seconds to lock the door behind me. Double-lock it.

Inside, I made my way to the bathroom, where I washed the blood off my leg, trying to make sure I didn't spatter any. I put a bandage on it and I crept to bed.

I looked at the clock. Past midnight. That made it Christmas morning.

I lay under my blankets, shivering with fear. Had I saved the rat or not? I think I had saved myself. I just didn't know.

CHRISTMAS

"Eric," my mom called. "You slug-a-bed! It's Christmas morning!"

I got up and checked the clock. It was almost nine-thirty. Considering what morning it was, that really was late.

I inspected my leg. There was a little blood, but actually it was just a scratch. No big deal.

We gathered around the tree.

Following tradition, my dad said, "Eric, open your sock first."

I went to it. It was stuffed, with a big orange—another tradition—poking out the top.

I lay the stocking on the coffee table. My folks stood around to watch me open it. Big smiles on their faces. The most common things were on the top, the best always at the bottom.

First came the orange. Then some nuts. A package of mechanical pencils. A Swiss Army knife. Candy, of course. Two tickets to a Yankee baseball game in the spring. I was getting close to the end. When I reached all of the way to the bottom I touched something soft and furry.

The rat.

Was it dead or alive?

I touched it again and . . . it moved.

I jerked my hand out of the stocking and held the top shut with two hands.

"Be right back!" I shouted.

"Eric! Where are you going?" Dad cried after me.

I didn't answer. I was down the elevator, into the lobby. I yanked the lobby door, then the front doors open and stepped outside. It must have been twenty degrees warmer than the day before. I mean, there were practically puddles on the sidewalk.

I went to the curb. Soon as I reached it I flipped the stocking over, shaking it.

The rat tumbled out.

For a moment, he just lay there in the gutter, as if dazed. Then he lifted his head and shook himself. Without even looking back at me, he scurried off.

Only when he had gone did I notice that a couple of things had fallen out with him.

One was a card of Anje's. On the back was written:

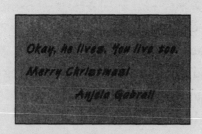

Okay, he lives. You live too.
Merry Christmas!
Anjela Gabrall

The other thing was the small white flashlight.

And later I was amazed again.

As we were walking to our Christmas dinner at the Willobys', my mother took my hand and squeezed it. "Thank you so much," she said softly.

"You mean for your present?" I said.

"That was nice. No, for the angel on the top of the tree. Eric, that was so sweet of you to fix it. It looks as good as it ever did."

When we got home I went into the living room

and looked up at the angel on the treetop. It was fixed, all right. Without the wings or robes, of course, our angel looked a little like Anje.

I laughed. It was Christmas day and I was alive—as I'd never been alive before. Felt great.

As for the flashlight, I've still got it. Sits on my bureau. Every once in a while—if I start feeling bored—it glows.

A Note about the Angel Gabriel

Gabriel is one of two angels named in the Bible. His name comes from the Hebrew, and, variously translated, means "the mighty one." He is also known as the "Prince of Fire." He is the angel of annunciation, mercy, vengeance, death, revelation, and resurrection.

In Jewish mythology Gabriel is connected to Adam's creation. It is also said he brought a glowing stone to Abraham for protection, the glow being the preserved light of the Garden of Eden, a source of wisdom and a shield.

In the New Testament it is Gabriel who announces the birth of Jesus to Mary. In this context he has a major association with Christmas. And it is Gabriel who will sound the trumpet for the Final Judgment.

In Islam, it's Gabriel who dictates the Koran to Muhammad. Muslims venerate him as a spirit of truth.

In *The Christmas Rat* I've taken bits and pieces from all these traditions.

As for Anje's phone number, it's in code. See if you can figure it out.

—Avi